The Slime Dungeon

Book 1
(The Slime Dungeon Chronicles)

Jeffrey "Falcon" Logue

Acknowledgements

To my family for believing in me

Cover and Design by Silvia Lew, my amazing illustrator
Gallery: http://www.silvialew.com/

Editor: Nora Logue

●●●

All work within this novel is fiction. All characters, places, and adventures were born within the mind of the author and have no relation to anything in real life.

This book is licensed for your personal enjoyment only; no copies should be made without the consent of the author. Thank you for respecting the author's hard work.

Text Copyright © 2016 Jeffrey "Falcon" Logue

All rights reserved

Table of Contents

Prologue i
Chapter 1 1
Chapter 2 15
Chapter 3 34
Chapter 4 52
Chapter 5 74
Chapter 6 87
Chapter 7 102
Chapter 8 115
Chapter 9 126
Chapter 10 143
Chapter 11 157
Chapter 12 170
Chapter 13 188
Chapter 14 204
Chapter 15 220
Chapter 16 244
Chapter 17 259
Chapter 18 275
Chapter 19 292
    City State Duran 305
    The Palace 310
    The Camp 316

Chapter 21 323
Chapter 22 342
Chapter 23 355
Chapter 24 377
Epilogue 405

Prologue

Someone is speaking to me; a woman, beautiful and full of life. Her visage fills my mind and leaves little for my own thoughts. She is smiling at me, but her countenance is sorrowful. Her beauty diminishes in her grief, and I don't like this. Memories flash through my mind, strange thoughts that don't give me comfort. A vision of something happening: laughter and lots of it. Another woman, smiling at me I think. I'm in a group, but I'm not sure. I know her name, yet it escapes me. I remember drinks, lots of them. I remember something about a celebration. It was a happy time, I think.

I remember walking with the group. I remember her smile. I remember the danger; no one noticing in time. I didn't drink as much. I remember pushing her away. Then, only pain was left. She was sad too, I think; I remember tears on her face. How strange, for it feels as an event from a long ago time ago, yet I feel like it was so very recent.

The beautiful lady is looking at me still. I think she was waiting for me to remember. Why is her smile so sad? Why is she sad? Is it for me? I feel fine, so she shouldn't be sad.

Oh, wait! I think I died. I guess that's something to be sad about, but I can't seem to feel it. The other girl makes me feel something though. I think it was happiness, the feeling I have. How strange; is it because she was saved by me? I'm happy she was okay.

Oh, the beauty is raising her arms. I feel myself start to fall away.

"Safe travels," she whispers to me.

I don't want to leave her. She makes me feel at peace, but I feel myself leaving her. The farther I fall, the more I forget her splendor. Her light disappears quickly, and I'm left alone in the darkness. How dark it is indeed, especially with the slight remembrance of her light.

All alone in the dark, my memories are fading fast now. I don't even have a name anymore. The knowledge I saw a lady is here, but her image is gone from my memory. I don't even remember if she was a she or not. It's all leaving me now. I refuse to let her face fade into the night as well; that other girl, her face is mine and mine alone. I save it, smothering it within myself as much as I can. Both images are saved in my soul: her smile, and her sadness. I think I managed to save them, but I don't even remember why now. I just know they were important to me, back when I dwelled within the light.

The darkness is disappearing, but there is still no light. I'm falling still, but more slowly now; slowly, slowly, slowly drifting down into a lighter darkness. All the way to a small source of light: a little crystal in the darkness, a twinkle in the night.

It brightens as I approach, and I feel myself drawn into it. It's warm, and comfortable like a home. It is now my home, I think; my home for my soul; a new body for me to live in. I don't remember my old body, yet I know the form my old body had at least for now. This one is new and interesting to me, being only a small crystal now. I wonder what I can do in it.

Now, though, I have to say my first words before I forget what words are. Well, as best as possible, I guess, with this body. I think I'll say her name, since I managed to hold on to it. It has a poetic feel to it after all: the first word should be the same as the last word: "Hannah."

Chapter 1

Lesson of Growth

Sometime after the fall I managed to fall asleep in my new body. Being reborn, I guess, was a truly interesting experience. I remembered nothing of emotional significance besides the two images, and I lost a lot of factual information as well. To put it in more simple terms, I was a blank slate with some leftover words left on it along with whatever lingering feelings dwelling alongside them.

Falling asleep in the new body was a lot different from what I can vaguely remember from my previous one. I had nothing to move, and no eyes to close. However, I felt my light die down as my consciousness faded away. My brightness was an indicator of my alertness, I guess, giving a whole new meaning to morning person. When I woke up, I found I could actively control the amount of light I gave off, and thus my level of alertness. It was actually kind of fun having control over my mind like that.

Once I finished doing that, I was left to figure out how I was, what I was, and how I should live now.

***

The 'newborn being' tested his new found limits from within his body. He could kind of sense the world around him with his light, and realized he could see images if he concentrated hard enough. There wasn't really anything to see however, because he was underground within the dirt and stone.

"Well, I'm a crystal that dwells in the dark," he thought to himself, "I wonder what I am."

Certainly, none of the faint memories could prepare him for this experience. His former life was almost all gone, but he was pretty sure he had been some sort of caregiver or healer. Among the little bits of knowledge remaining dwelt the impressions of bodies he could only vaguely imagine.

"Given that only that which I felt important remains with me, I can only assume being a healer was a large part of my life. In any case, none of it seems to apply to my current situation nor provides useful input to my situation."

He took a moment to laugh at his word usage; another aspect of his former existence that he felt slowly disappearing.

The being checked his body again. He was a small crystal, his mind referencing him as about inch tall and half an inch wide. His shape was of an octagon with pyramid shapes on both ends, making him some sort of prism. He gave off a soft purple light that fed him information about his surroundings. He could not maintain the light at full intensity too long, and had to rest after sensing for a while.

"Well, I wonder what I can do with the light besides looking."

The being focused on what he assumed to be the front of his body. The light dimmed around him and focused into the area he was concentrating on. A small beam of purple light shot forth from his body and began to create a hole in front of him.

"Jackpot!" The being thought happily, "Now I can focus on something."

The beam didn't go too far, and he felt tired after concentrating for a while.

"Guess I have to rest more often if I want to do more work." He sighed to himself. He observed the small hole he had made. It was circular and went about an inch in front of his body. The walls of the hole were different from the rest of the dirt, seemingly fused together into a purple stone that would not collapse.

The being smiled as a memory came to him, the last one he would have of his former life. "This will be my home." He thought inwardly. "I will carve out my living here and I will survive."

The being adopted a routine of work and rest that he followed for the next few weeks. He would dig until he slept, wake up, and continue to dig with his light. Not wanting to fall to the floor, he focused on creating a room with his crystal in the far wall. It took almost a month, but he managed to create a small 4 by 4 room that he became quite proud of.

"Now, let's see what else there is to do."

The being had been trying to figure out how he functioned while he worked on his room. He had managed to use enough power to keep himself barely awake instead of fully unconscious, and had found his body absorbing something from the surroundings. It resembled a blue energy of some type, and it had flowed into his body to become purple light within him, filling him up with energy.

"Okay, here I go." He concentrated on the feeling again, trying to absorb the energy into him. He felt the pull of light from his body, then lost it all as it faded into exhaustion. The last few tests had ended the same, resulting in him falling asleep from the exertion. It annoyed him to no end that he could do something easier asleep than awake. "Why isn't it working?" He groaned. "I can feel the energy, but I can't bring it in."

After failing previous tests, the being had learned how to keep a minimal level of energy that prevented him from falling asleep. Once again, he watched the blue energy flow into him as he rested and proceeded to growl at it.

"What kind of energy is easier to use when asleep?" He complained, "How am I supposed to survive without any knowledge about living? There is something obvious that I am missing from this..."

As he thought this, the blue energy stopped flowing into him and instead flowed in front of him. It condensed together into a blue box and, much to his surprise, began displaying words he could understand.

> Conditions for sentience satisfied
>
> Beginning start up sequence...
>
> Welcome to the world

The being was surprised beyond words, so it was expected that his response was not the most elegant of phrases. "Wh... hell is this crap?" The blue box didn't indicate an emotional response, but its words were quite clear.

> How rude, is this how you treat all your friends?

"I have no idea, since I don't have any," he retorted to the funny blue box. "What are you and why are you made of my food?"

The blue box vibrated with what the being suspected was laughter.

> How amusing! Well, to answer your questions: I am a spirit whose purpose is to help you. You may call me Claire or Clarence.
>
> Your "food," as you call it, is actually mana, and I am using it to talk to you because you are currently underground and have no available space for me to speak with you directly.

The being examined the box a moment before replying,

"Hate to burst your bubble, but I have a room you can be in. Can I have my, err, mana back?"

The blue box was blank for a moment before it faded back into the blue light and resumed its path toward his crystal. A small blue hole appeared in his room and out of it a small winged figure appeared.

The being had never seen this creature before; it was small with four appendages in pairs on the sides of its body with some wispy material on its head. He had vaguely recalled the words "hair," "legs," and "arms" before the creature began speaking.

"My goodness! The winged figure said, looking around. "You have been quite busy haven't you? I didn't even know dungeons could do this before proper induction."

The being was a little annoyed still about his mana being interrupted. "I don't know what you are implying, but I worked hard to do all this you know. I don't need little annoyances coming in and stealing my food. I almost passed out because of the delay." He focused his light in its direction and asked, "What are you anyway?"

The winged figure flew up and hovered in front of the being with its hands crossed. "You're a rude one, aren't you? Well, I guess I'd be a little upset too if I was just born alone a few days ago and had someone steal my nourishment."

"A few days!? It's been weeks since I was born," the being said with a confused tone, "Are you in the right place?" The tiny being froze and slowly drifted to the ground. She/he looked around the room slowly and took in the purple covered walls.

"Are you telling me you've been carving this entire room by yourself for weeks now without any guidance?" The winged figure asked slowly.

That's about right; I've experimented some with that... err... mana, and figured out how to make the room. I was trying to figure out how to process mana faster when you showed up."

The little thing put its hands over its face. "I can't believe this, my first assignment and I'm already messing up." It began to cry, which made the crystal being very uncomfortable.

"Okay, um, please stop crying. What's wrong?"

The tiny being sniffled and sobbed, "But, I was supposed to take care of you, and, and I messed up... waahhh!"

The being was really confused now, and slightly annoyed at the revelation. The crying continued, "[Sniff] I'm a dungeon pixie. We are born in dungeons and live together with them. When a dungeon pixie becomes of age, we go out and search for a new dungeon to raise and teach so it can become a new home. [Sniff], Mommy told me she didn't expect me to find a dungeon and that I could stay with her forever, but I told her I could handle it myself and on my own. But... but, you don't need me anymore... wahhhhhhh!"

The being was sympathetic now. He understood the need for independence and the hardships of trying to forge a place in the world for oneself. After all, that was what he had been doing the past few weeks. "It's okay, you know," he said, "I only know this stuff and nothing else. I could really use your help to make myself a better dungeon, if that is what I am."

The pixie sniffed, looking up from the floor with wide eyes, "Really? You want me to stay with you?"

The being slowly smiled, not that she could see him do so, and said, "Sure, I think I'll enjoy having someone show me the ropes. Welcome to my dungeon; or start of one anyway."

With a happy cry, the pixie flew up and hugged the crystal with its body. He was startled for a moment because it was the same size as him, and its glow turned slightly red for a moment. The glow was a reflex though, for he did not know how to react to this sudden show of affection. The pixie let go and pointed at the wall below the crystal. A small perch stretched out from the wall, and it landed on it and bowed.

"Thank you very much for allowing me a home Mr. Dungeon. First things first, though; do you want me to be Claire or Clarence?"

"Does it matter?" The pixie nodded, "Dungeon pixies are born gender neutral and given two names until they bond with a dungeon crystal. You'll determine my gender for the rest of my life as well as a small part of my personality. At the same time, I get to pick out a name for you. That creates our bond, and I won't have to read your mind to talk to you anymore."

"Oh, I was wondering how you heard me. We'll be linked through our minds then?" The pixie nodded. "Yes, but it will just allow normal talking. We won't be able to read each other's mind." The being mentally nodded, "Well then, I name you Claire, the Dungeon Pixie." Claire smiled at him, "And I name you Doc, the Dungeon Heart."

Doc's purple light focused between the two and they felt their minds being connected to each other.

And that was the beginning of the relationship between Claire, the Dungeon Pixie, and Doc the Dungeon Heart.

Chapter 2

After they established their bond, Doc and Claire both fell asleep; with Claire sleeping with the back of Doc's crystal body. Their sleep was peaceful, uneventful, and revitalizing to both of them. They woke up at the same time and sent each other happy thoughts as they beheld each other.

"Good morning Doc." Claire said happily. "Good morning Claire." He responded with equal enthusiasm. "Did you sleep well?"

She nodded and began flying around in front of him. "Mommy always told me the best sleep would come after a binding, but I never imagined I would feel this good!" She giggled and did a little jig in front of his body, "I feel so rested and full of energy!"

Doc gave her a chuckle, "I feel the same way. Now, what is next for us to do?"

Claire landed on the little wall extension and created a chair and table out of the stone in front of

Doc's body. She sat down and smiled at him cutely. "Why, now its Q and A time, my silly Doc. Feel free to ask me anything and everything your crystal mind wants to know." She giggled again, "This is so exciting!"

Doc chuckled to himself. His new friend sure was an adorable little thing. "What am I?" He asked her firmly.

Claire pointed at his body, "You are a dungeon; a being whose main body is that of a crystal. Your magic allows you to control the territory around you and change it to suit your needs. The reason why those like you are called dungeons is because of your tendency to create great caves and labyrinths in the earth which hide countless treasures and monsters. What else do you want to know?"

Satisfied and intrigued by his race's namesake, Doc asked, "Okay, then, explain to me this bond thing."

Claire nodded, "Sure, I'll do my best." She folded her hands in front of her on the table, but couldn't quite pull off the professional look she was going for. "The bond between a dungeon heart and a dungeon pixie is very unique in this world. We connect spiritually in such a way we always know where the other is located and can talk to each other from any location. Beyond that, we can't harm each other. I have a limited control over a part of your dungeon. That area will serve as my personal home and resting place."

Sensing his emotions, she quickly corrected herself, "I don't mean anything big in your dungeon. I just have enough influence to create a home and other things for myself, like this table and chair." She pointed down at the objects made of purple stone.

"Also, our bond will increase the amount of mana you absorb from the environment because I'm a magic being that also uses mana from the surroundings. You should be able to absorb mana passively now whenever you feel like it."

Checking, Doc confirmed he could adjust the pull of mana now without becoming tired. "I see that. Why couldn't I do that before?"

"Silly! It's because you are not a magic creature. You are a crystal that can use mana, a more special type of a soul gem. A soul gem has a natural ability to store mana, but can't use it on its own. Under certain circumstances, however, a soul gem can evolve into a heart crystal like yourself and gain the ability to use mana. Suffice to say, most young dungeons try to absorb as much mana as possible as they wake up. When they reach their limit, we dungeon pixies pick up on their needs and use our abilities to communicate with them in order to form a bond. That's why I was upset when I came here; I thought you didn't need me which meant that I would be alone forever."

"Explain this to me: Is the dungeon connection unique?"

Claire nodded, "Yup. A dungeon pixie gets one chance to bind with a dungeon. If one fails, then they have to live the rest of their lives alone...not that we can live long without a dungeon." She frowned and let some tears fall from her eyes. "Mommy told me Daddy got a late signal in his life, but before he could bond, adventurers had already found his partner and killed him. I never met him."

While feeling sympathetic, Doc sensed danger in her words. "A dungeon can be killed? Am I in danger?"

Claire looked up and shook her head, wiping her tears away. "Not right now. Daddy's crystal was too close to another established dungeon. When it was conquered, they searched the area and took everything valuable. Right now we are deep underground with nothing near us so there is no danger."

Doc regarded his body curiously, "So I'm valuable to adventurers? What are adventurers anyway?"

Claire giggled, forgetting her sadness, "Yup, even a small crystal like you is important because you can absorb mana. Soul gems are used in powerful weapons, spells, and armor, so they are very valuable."

"What's a weapon?"

"Something to be learned later," Claire admitted. "Anyway, the bigger your body gets, the stronger your dungeon will be. To answer your other question, there are big people in the world that work and live together. Humans, dwarves, elves, demonoids, gnomes, beast-men, and other races live and compete against each other. Adventurers can be any race, and they do things for other member of their race. Some of the things they do include activities like dungeon diving."

"Why do they do things for others?" Doc asked curiously, "Do they have bonds between them too?"

This gave Claire a large fit of giggled as she rolled onto the floor. She quickly recovered and coughed in embarrassment. "Like I said before, only dungeon and dungeon pixies have that kind of bond. Adventurers do things in order to gain one of three things: wealth, fame, and adventure. Most will die in their line of work, but they all strive toward these three things. You do understand what those things are, right?" Claire asked cautiously.

"I think I do, though I'm not sure why," Doc admitted to her, "So am I expected to die to these adventurers?"

Claire shook her head, "No, there is no need for you to die to them; in fact, it is my desire that we both live and prosper for many years. Most adventurers should just come in and take a treasure or monster loot from you and leave you alone as long as you don't do dumb things like killing everything in sight. Long term, dungeons are a great way to make profit as long as they exist, so don't expect too much danger once a lot of people know about you."

Doc nodded, "Okay then, so how do I become a well-known dungeon?"

Claire, smiling, sat on the table with her legs crossed and her hands on her knee. Doc couldn't help but notice her growing femininity now that she was named. It didn't help she was dressed in a purple dress with a petal like skirt. "That's the fun part Doc, now we get to decide what you'll be."

Claire waved her finger again, and the blue mana formed another blue screen in front of Doc's face.

Choose your desired starting race:
Goblin
Common staring monster. Monsters with a closer connection to sentient

races. Fast breeders. Possess average intelligence. Evolution path varied and defined.
Kobold
Common starting monster. Lowest monster race with draconian blood. Mainly found near great wyrms' homes. Average breeders. Possess higher than average intelligence. Evolution path is set and undefined.
Orc
Uncommon starting monsters.

- Long lineage of fighting sentient races.
- Dungeon Orcs are different from their regular Orc cousins who live in semi-peace with the other sentient races.
- Brutal and cunning.
- Fast breeders.
- Initially much stronger than other starting monster races.
- Evolution path is short and defined.

Imp

- Uncommon starting monsters.
- Lowest form of demons.
- Found near underworld portals and/or lava.
- Average breeders.
- Possess great cunning, but little physical

prowess.

Evolution path is varied and defined.

Animal

Common starting monster.

Variety of starting choices.

Breeding speed species dependent.

Evolves quickly.

Evolution path is undefined.

Slime

Rare starting monster.

Lacking intelligence and speed.

Slow breeders.

Evolution path is varied and undefined

Doc blinked at the very large blue screen of mana in front of his face. "Claire, what is this?"

She fluttered up beside the screen, "To start a good dungeon, you need monsters. Monster will both protect your core and add an incentive to not kill you by dropping loot and treasure. Allow me to answer more questions before we look into this some more."

Doc frowned, "Okay, but how do I make the treasure and monsters appear out of thin air? I don't have any treasure beside my own body, and I'd prefer not giving that up."

Claire nodded, "Right, but there are things we can do to make treasure." She pointed at the walls of his room, "As you can see, your magic infuses mana and transforms the stone into a part of your dungeon. In essence, that wall is now a part of you. The extent of your territory is determined by your crystal's size."

She flew over to a section of the wall on his right, "Here is your first lesson: concentrate your mana here and focus on gold. Picture it in your mind and focus all those thoughts here."

Doc nodded and then paused. "I have never seen gold before," he said apologetically.

Claire nodded, and then took a small coin from her skirt. It glittered gold under the purple light. "This is a small piece of gold," she explained. "It is one form of currency used by all races, though pixie gold is a lot smaller than other sentient gold coins. Examine it, then try to make it."

Doc huffed, then followed her orders. He felt his purple light leaving his body and concentrated around the area she had pointed to. As he pictured the gold in his head, he was surprised to find his light disappearing. Feeling nervous at the unexpected loss, he quickly stopped and felt the light return to his body.

Claire flew over to him, frowning, and asked: "Why did you stop? You didn't make much at all," she complained to him as she glanced at the wall.

"What happened just now? I felt my mana disappearing." Doc asked nervously. Unlike Claire, he could not see the effects of his mana's loss and was loathed to lose any of it. All this new information had made him tense, especially when learning about death. He wasn't a crystal that would fill with fear at the first sign of trouble, but he was trying to be cautious about alerting the dangerous adventurers of his presence.

Claire huffed, "As I thought, you've only used your magic to carve and destroy rather than create. I bet not seeing results made you nervous, right?"

"Hey, I made this room, didn't I?" Doc said defensively, "Am I wrong to take things slow and steady?"

She waved her hand, "Making a room was easy for you because you dissolved all the stone you didn't want. The reluctance you felt is actually one of your dungeon instincts kicking in. Crystals naturally horde their mana, so it's a hard lesson to teach new dungeons how to overcome their instincts. Try looking at what's behind the wall now."

Doc sensed the area and was surprised. "Is that gold?" Within the wall, out of sight, the area was intermingled with tiny gold specs that glistened in the purple light. Not enough to be called a proper vein; however, it was enough to garner interest from anyone who saw it.

Claire nodded, "Yup. That is gold you created with your own power. It is magic completely unique to dungeons. They can create minerals and monsters within themselves by using the mana created by their bodies. The strongest mages can cast a lesser form after years of accumulating power and experience, but to dungeons it is an innate ability. That ability only works when the dungeon is alive, and is impossible to be replicated by any mortal. As you just experienced, you can only create metals and stones that you understand and examine; I have some copper and iron on me as well so feel free to look at them at your leisure. When you get strong enough, you can create areas that are full of metal to be mined by adventurers."

Doc nodded, "Okay, so I can create areas to be mined. Should I do so now throughout the dungeon?"

"NOOOO!!!!" Doc was surprised by Claire's frantic scream as she flew in front of him frantically. "Remember how I said the walls are a part of you? Well, imagine if thousands of greedy adventurers were mining your body every day and every hour searching for gold."

The purple crystal actually turned slightly white for a moment as Doc processed the information. "Okay, so I don't make my entire dungeon a mine then; how about a small area?"

Claire calmed down and took her seat, "Yes, you can have specialized areas for mining, but don't make the entire dungeon like that, okay?" Feeling his agreement, she sighed in relief. "Also, since my house will be hidden in your walls, I don't want miners to find me. Dungeon pixies are a rare commodity that slave traders like to hunt, and most die after being captured. Anyway, as I was saying, your walls can form the metals and you can absorb them into your astral body."

"My what?" Doc asked, confused.

Claire pointed over to his body, "Think of it as an invisible bag only you can access. Within your dungeon, you can take anything not attached to another being. For instance, if an idiot adventurer dies inside you, feel free to absorb his belongings and body. His valuables can be given to your monsters as loot and his body can be made into a skeleton or zombie if you desire."

Claire grimaced, "I won't protest too much, but I don't like zombie dungeons. They get really smelly and make the Church priests angry and vengeful."

"What is the Church?" He asked her.

"Not important right now," Claire answered. "Any other questions for me?"

Doc nodded, "Yeah, what do you mean give loot to monsters? Also, how do I get monsters?"

"To answer both questions, monsters within a dungeon fall into two types: natural and dungeon born. Natural monsters wander in from the outside and co-exist with the dungeon, like me technically. Dungeon born monsters are not alive; they are merely projections of your mana into a solid form that obey the same rules as regular monsters. When they die, their mana returns to you and they leave behind loot: sometimes a body part of value, or sometimes you can add the loot from your astral bag. The astral bag will summon out an appropriate item as loot once it is assigned to your monsters.

Doc chuckled, "You know Claire, sometimes you are the smartest in the room, and other times you are like a little child. It's very cute to watch."

Claire blushed, "Dungeon pixies dream of bonding their entire lives, so we learn as much as we can to make our dungeons happy. A pixie can only have one dungeon, but a dungeon can replace the pixie at any time." She gave him her cute, pout stare, "You promise never to replace me?"

Doc nodded, "Yes, we'll be friends forever."

She giggled and cried, "Hooray for Doc!" as she flew around the room. As she settled back down, she smiled and asked, "Okay Doc, which race do you want as your first monster?"

Doc snorted, "Isn't it obvious? Let's go with Kobold!"

Chapter 3

Claire smiled at him and nodded in approval, "Great choice! Kobolds are a very easy race to deal with and have lots of possible evolutions."

Doc nodded, "Yup. There is nothing cooler than having dragons in a dungeon."

A silence filled the room.

Claire stared up at him and began to cough awkwardly. Doc regarded her with the crystal equivalent of a raised eyebrow. "Is something the matter?" He asked pointedly.

"... not..."

"What was that?"

"I'm sorry that won't be possible." Claire said apologetically.

Doc felt his spirits falter, "Why can't I have dragons? Kobolds have dragon blood and can evolve right? So why can't I have dragons?" He felt a little childish, but he really wanted some dragons in his dungeon. He had a rather strong impression that if he had dragons, he wouldn't have to be worried about anyone conquering him.

Claire gave him a pitying look, "Well, it's not possible because dragons are like dungeon pixies; they are magic beings and very mighty ones at that. Even the weakest true dragons are way stronger than most things in this world, and dungeons cannot create anything stronger than themselves. Only monsters can be made, and until you reach a certain level of strength, you can only make simple ones. It's possible to evolve them later on, but that's more of an evolution of your mana capacity rather than the monsters themselves. Do you get it?"

Doc nodded remorsefully. He understood the implications of creating things that could kill the creator, namely him, but that didn't mean he was happy about it.

"Fine," he muttered, "Then I choose slimes."

Claire winced visibly at his words, "Are you sure Doc? No dungeon, in my extensive research, has ever chosen slimes because of how awkward they are to have at the beginning."

"It's an option isn't it? That means it's a viable choice for dungeons and a common monster."

Claire nodded haltingly, "Yes, but slimes are never the first race in a dungeon; they are normally an "add on" for variety in the dungeon. Even in the wild, slimes normally never get the chance to become strong because they are so easily killed by magic; however," Claire reluctantly admitted, "The slimes that do survive are tough to deal with, I admit, especially when they evolve out of their slime form."

Doc perked up at this, "What do you mean by "evolve out?" Can they become other races?"

Claire huffed, seeing that Doc wouldn't be dissuaded, "Well, the most dangerous evolution I know of would be the gelatinous slimes. Those monsters are extremely dangerous because they are impervious to physical weapons and can easily change shape from a puddle to a cube the size of a man in an instant. They have an annoying ability to split every once in a while and create new ones. The worst part is that they are completely immune to physical attacks of any form. Very few of those exist because armies are called to destroy the area when one pops up; they are considered that much of a menace."

"Great, let's do that!" Doc said happily.

Claire marched through the air to his body and glared at him, her hands on her hips, "Didn't we agree making others angry was a bad life decision?"

Doc shrugged, "That's a long way off, right? Besides, as long as the dangerous ones are deep in my dungeon, it won't be dangerous to anyone besides the adventurers, right? In fact, I bet those adventurers would see it as a bit of a challenge. Can a dungeon monster leave the dungeon?"

Claire mulled over it for a moment, "The majority of dungeon-born monsters cannot leave their home dungeon. Besides that, everything else you've said is true. But I have to ask," she gave him pleading eyes, "Why can't it be animals? Cute, fluffy, adorable animals that I can hug and love and sleep on?"

Doc carefully maintained a neutral façade over his "face," "Because you would be broken up every time one of them dies?"

Claire paused, and then drooped sadly, "Oh, you're right. Okay then, slimes it is." She stared up sheepishly, "At least you didn't choose undead."

Doc stared at her, "I didn't see that option."

Claire coughed and turned around, "Right, slimes it is then. Let me just finalize this."

"Hold on, did you hide a choice from me?" Doc asked.

Claire waved her hands and Doc felt his entire being shudder for a moment. "Great! You can create slime minions now."

Doc stared at her for a moment and asked her again, "Did you hide a choice form me?"

"Maybe?"

"Claire!"

She pouted, "Yes."

"Why?"

"Zombies smell bad."

"Your birth place was a zombie dungeon, huh?"

"... Yes."

Doc sighed, "Its fine, I guess; just don't lie to me again, okay?"

Claire nodded, but Doc sensed a little mischievousness from her. "Whatever you say Doc, you're the boss." She turned around and smiled at him, "Now, hurry up and make your first monster!"

"Okay, how do I do that?" He inquired eagerly.

Claire pointed at the ground, "Well, it is very similar to how you made the gold earlier. Focus your mana and imagine a slime."

Doc gave her a droll look, "Really! Then, what does a slime look like?"

Claire paused, then drooped, "Well, I was hoping you would know. I learned a lot, but never with pictures. My mommy's dungeon didn't have any either."

Doc mentally patted her head, "Well, what is the description of a slime?"

Claire tilted her head and recited, "A basic slime is a small viscous blob made of a liquid-like material with a core inside it. The core acts like a heart, using mana to keep the slime body intact and in motion. Colors usually depict the type of slime, but most experts agree a newborn slime is clear until it eats its first meal. For a basic slime, color depicts the attribute it has the most affinity to and it reveals its evolution pathway."

Doc nodded, "So a slime is a core surrounded by 'slime,' right? I can picture that." He concentrated on the middle of the room and focused his magic. Like before, he felt his mana draining as his magic gave birth to his first monster. From the center of the room, a small black stone arose and began secreting slime around itself. Quickly, it wobbled up to its fullest slime height and began moving across the floor.

Claire clapped happily and flew down to the slime, poking it with her feet as it moved slowly. "Congratulations, you made a slime!"

Doc smiled happily, "Thanks, but why is it purple?" The slime was clear, but it possessed a purple tint as it oozed around.

"That's because you made it, silly. Your mana is purple, so it is purplish." She answered simply.

"Oh, good to know... Isn't it dangerous for you to be touching it like that? Won't it eat you?"

Claire giggled, "Nope! You and I are bonded so we can't hurt each other, and all your monsters are extensions of you. In fact, I think I found my new bed." With a yawn, she fell asleep on top of the slime.

Doc chuckled to himself. "I may not need sleep, but I guess she still does." He thought as he regarded the little pixie with affection. "That slime does look comfortable, so I am a little jealous." The slime in question ignored everything as it moved across the floor.

"I guess I can't talk to my creatures then." He sighed, 'Then again, I wonder if I can evolve them to be more intelligent?" From what Claire had said, no one had ever really used slimes up to their full potential, and Doc was itching for a challenge. First thing he needed to do, though, was to make more slimes.

The initial slime didn't use much of his mana, so he went ahead and made nine more. The ten slimes were oozing across the floor soon after, and Doc chuckled as he watched Claire snoozing in a den of slime.

He decided to note the behavior of the slimes for future reference: Basic slimes were small, maybe a liter in size; they could stick to everything in his room, from the floor to the ceiling. When two slimes bumped into each other, they giggled and bounced apart, then moved in opposite directions. To Doc, it was like watching little balls bouncing off each other. The slimes themselves didn't seem to be growing much at all, but their light purple color seemed to be turning deeper. Doc assumed it was because they were feeding on his essence from the stones around him.

Doc decided he was tired of a single room. While interacting with Claire, he had been silently sensing the world around him, and it turned out he was closer to the outside world than she had thought. Granted, he didn't want to open a tunnel straight to his body, but he did want an opening to feel the outside air, metaphorically speaking, of course.

To his delight, he found that the slimes were absorbing, on their own, mana from the environment on their own, and he could use what they absorbed for himself. He focused on making a small hole to the surface, a mere 1 by 1 square tunnel to connect his body to the outside. With his new mana sources and increased absorption rate, he had no problem focusing his magic into the form he wanted, and shot it toward the surface.

Unfortunately, his focus literally shot the magic up and out, using up all of his mana till he was barely conscious. Even without his mana adding to it, the magical disintegrating blast continued until it burst out into the fresh air and exploded in a loud pop of stone and dirt.

The noise woke Claire up causing her to fall off her slime. In a panic, she started flying around wildly.

"What was that? Was it an explosion? Are we being invaded so soon? What's going on?" She turned to Doc and noted his condition. Eyes narrowed, she flew over to him and gave him a terrifying glare. "What did you do?"

Doc sheepishly said, "Oops."

After Doc's explanation, Claire left immediately to survey the extent of the damage. She sent him results when she reached the new entrance.

Apparently, the spell had continued after Doc's loss of control and continued in the original direction. However, instead of breaking down the rock and dirt, it had instead pushed it out of the way, resulting in an explosion that created havoc all around and a crater with a small hole in the middle. The tunnel itself was pretty long, but narrow. Claire was extremely frustrated with Doc, but she grudgingly admitted that he had surely made a showy entrance. Apparently, dungeons that hid themselves were considered suspicious by the adventurers and were more often killed. While Claire didn't see any nearby signs of one of the sentient races, the sound would have carried for a long distance.

"I can't believe you did something so foolish without my help. Don't you realize we're partners in this?" Doc wasn't sure if Claire was more upset with being left out or having their existence revealed so soon.

"Well, what's the next step since we have completed this one?"

'You mean you finished' Claire muttered angrily under her breath. Sighing, she took her seat in front of Doc and put her head in her hands.

"Normally, we'd practice your room creation and focus on improving yourself slowly, but now we don't have the luxury of time anymore." She looked up, "Now, we have to work on defenses and rewards."

Doc sent her a confused feeling, "The tunnel is really small though, isn't it? Are the adventurers so small they can fit inside?"

Claire chuckled and shook her head, "No, not at all. Most adventurers are a few feet bigger than this room. However, it's in poor form to leave the entrance so small after announcing our existence, so we'll have to enlarge it to accommodate them."

"The suspicious presentation thing again?" He asked for conformation.

She nodded, "Yup, we don't want to look like we're hiding anything. You have to enlarge the entrance, tunnels, and the heart room."

Doc shuddered nervously, "I don't want adventurers in this room though."

Claire nodded sadly, "I agree, but we don't have a choice. You're too weak to have hidden rooms, so we can't hide anything yet. For now, this room serves as the final boss room."

"Can I at least hide my body?"

Claire nodded, "You can for now. The area where a dungeon is born always becomes the dungeon's heart room and you'll never leave here by choice. It's the place where your mana is most concentrated and pure, so eventually you will float in the center of the room without hiding. For now, however, you are small enough to hide in the wall."

Focusing, Doc moved the room's stone over his crystal body. Now, he was completely hidden from prying eyes.

Claire sighed, "That was my biggest worry, and I can feel better about your safety now. How do you feel?"

"Like I just pushed my body to the limits," he said honestly.

Claire nodded, eyeing the slimes in the room. "At least you made enough slimes before blasting through the stone; they are a big help in recovering mana for you. Go ahead and make ten more just to be safe."

Making ten more slimes was still easy for him, so Doc went ahead and focused his power. The new slimes quickly got to work and soon Doc felt his mana levels rising steadily.

"This is great; my mana is almost full again," he said happily.

"Be careful, though," Claire cautioned, "Slimes are easy to make and easy to kill with anything magical. When adventurers are in your dungeon, you'll learn that it takes a lot of mana to create new monsters. An adventurer's innate life will interfere with your abilities and make it difficult to directly attack them with anything. In fact, it is impossible to change your dungeon around while others are in it due to the strain it would place on you. Try it and the process would drain you completely dry and kill you."

"Why is it like that? Do the adventurers have some magic limiting ability that interferes with me?" Claire waved her hand back and forth, "It's actually protection given to all sentient beings who pray to a higher divinity or any creatures under the protection of a deity. They don't want their followers and chosen creatures to be slaughtered mercilessly unless special conditions are satisfied."

Doc nodded, "So it makes it fairer to adventurers then? I guess that makes sense. Is that what the church is connected to?"

Claire frowned, "Yes, but let's worry about that subject later."

Doc mentally shrugged, "Okay then Claire, whatever you say. Now, what kind of defenses can I make?"

Claire pointed at the slimes, "Anything that uses slimes would be good. Pitfalls, ceiling drops, and puddle ambushes are the best ways to use slimes.

The last two are things slimes can do on their own, but you'll have to make the pitfalls in your floor."

Doc regarded her in surprise, "I thought slimes weren't intelligent enough for complicated things"

Claire shook her head, "They may lack any intelligence, but this is instinct for them; nothing smart about it. Now, time to get to work!"

Chapter 4

Doc was completely exhausted. Claire had constantly been pushing him to finalize their dungeon. Unlike her normal demeanor, Claire was all business now that the dungeon was exposed for the entire world to see and explore. It was a strange contrast to her previous childlike behavior, but Doc attributed it to the nature of the situation.

She had Doc enlarge spaces along the tunnel to form rooms. She had kept a hawk's eye on his mana levels and concentration; she barked orders when he started to slip and making sure his mana never fell below conscious level. When he got low, she made him switch to creating more slimes, never allowing him to rest for a second. When she required sleep, she gave Doc a task to complete before she woke up and then settled on top of a slime. After the simple rooms were carved out, she had him enlarge the corridors to six feet in height and four feet from wall to wall. Doc kept his complaints down to a minimum because in no way could he avoid responsibility for his actions.

He didn't know if crystals could become sore, but he was fairly sure he felt what that would be like.

"Oh, hush up you!" Claire scolded, "You have enough slimes now to never sleep, what's the problem?"

"I never realized how much I missed sleep until this moment," Doc retorted, "You haven't let me rest in five days!"

Claire snorted, "Oh, please! I know dungeons don't need rest like other creatures. You're just lazy and young. How would you know what sleep is anyway?"

Doc paused, "I know I had memories of sleep; well, maybe. Being asleep means one does not know what's going on around them right?"

Claire flew back to her table and lay across it, gazing at him. "Yes, but in a more resting manner than what you have experienced. It's interesting, though, because most dungeons are newborns and have no knowledge of anything, and yet, you seem familiar with some topics you've never learned. I'm interested to see how being with you changes over time since I'm sure you're an old soul."

"Old soul, what's that?" He asked questioningly.

Claire rolled over, "Well, remember how I told you dungeons arise from variant soul gems? Soul gems have been used in the past to hold souls long after the body had turned to dust. Occasionally, a newly formed dungeon heart might accidentally pick up a departing soul and trap it within itself. During the process, a lot of experience from the past life may be lost, so no matter what, all dungeons need to be taught things. Now, most souls cannot be trapped this way due to the protection provided by the gods unless they lost it somehow. Evil criminals are the most common case, which supports the natural view that most dungeons are malicious. Good souls are rarer, I think you are one of them."

"So, does that make me unique?"

Claire shook her head, "Nope, you have all the powers and limits of a regular dungeon. The only things special about you would be your understanding of things you can't experience, like sleep. Well, you also get to bypass the multiple stages needed to become sentient, so I guess that's a bonus."

I also remember 'her,' though, Doc thought, if nothing else, I'll always remember her. His mind jerked back to reality as Claire began hitting the stone he was hidden behind.

"No distractions now, hurry up and finish the entrance and the pitfalls."

Sighing, Doc returned to his previous task. Claire wanted a large and showy entrance to welcome visitors, but Doc wanted something simpler for the task. They'd been arguing the last day about it, but they'd set it aside and had settled on the pitfall traps first.

The traps were pretty easy for him to make. He moved a section of his floor to form a hole, and let a few slimes drop in. Then he covered it with a thin stone designed to support the weight of small things like slimes and nothing else. The dungeon was pretty simple, given the time they had: Three large rooms and his room at the end with pitfall traps sprinkled in the tunnels. He had about seventy simple slimes, and they were now everywhere. Almost understanding what he was doing, the slimes had gone into the pits on their own, turned into puddles, or had climbed up to the ceiling and blended in to the stone.

"They have pretty good instincts," he commented as the last slime rolled into his pit.

Claire shrugged, "I'd say it was more you than them, but whatever you say." She was back on top of his first slime, which had become her favorite place to lie down. This slime was the darkest purple and never moved far from his room.

"So Claire, what's the story with this slime?" Doc asked, indicating her moving bed.

Claire smiled, "Oh! This slime? This is you."

Doc was confused, "But I'm me."

Claire giggled, "No, silly, I mean this is your other body." She flew around the slime and pointed, "This is your dungeon boss."

She held up her hand, "Yes, I know you have no idea what a dungeon boss is, so I'll go ahead and tell you. A dungeon boss is how it sounds; the boss of your dungeon. Normally, it is your first monster or the monster that has survived the longest. It has the strongest connection to you, so after you designate it and infuse it with your power, it will become a body you can possess and fight with."

"So I'm not stuck as a crystal then? I can move around in that slime?" Doc asked excitedly.

Claire gave him thumbs up, "Right! This is also the last step of making a dungeon, besides the entrance. Right now this is simple slime, but if you push your will into it, it will grow to become your boss. In fact, go ahead and give it a go!"

Claire flew up to her chair to watch the action while Doc got to work. He focused on the slime and pushed, but felt nothing happening. "Claire, it's not working," he informed her.

"You aren't creating something silly, so stop using mana. Use your mind instead to possess it."

Feeling embarrassed, Doc tried again, this time pushing himself into the slime. He felt his conscious drawn out of his crystal; pass through his walls down to the slime. Experiencing vertigo, he watched in amazement as the slime rumbled and grew quickly. Soon, it was big enough to cover a good bit of the floor and very purple in coloration. Doc felt his awareness switch from the wall to the floor, and realized he could feel things.

Being a slime was a very different experience for him. He couldn't feel his dungeon as well as before, but was more conscious of the surface he was touching. Moving was also a new experience, and he enjoyed rolling his mass across the floor. Claire flew down and plopped onto his head.

"So, what do you think?"

"Blurb, blub, blub," Doc answered. Startled, he found he couldn't talk the same way as he could before.

Claire giggled so hard she fell off his head. "Sorry about that, I forgot to mention you can't speak like you're used to whenever you are in your dungeon's boss body. I can hear your thoughts though, so go with that."

This is cool Claire. He thought happily, now I can explore my own dungeon.

"Oh no, you don't!" Claire scolded, "Hurry and leave so you can finish the entrance."

Grumbling, Doc left his new body and returned to his crystal. "Fine, but I still think the entrance should be simple."

Claire folded her arms, "A grand entrance will make sure everyone knows we aren't hiding anything."

"It could also be perceived as a trap to lure in fools." Doc countered, "A simple entrance may look like a trap, but at least it's honest."

Claire sighed and shrugged, "Oh fine, then, but it still has to be obvious that it's a dungeon entrance okay?"

"Okay." Doc moved his awareness to the front of the dungeon and gazed at his entrance. At the moment, it was still the small round hole with a large corridor behind it. Using his magic, Doc removed the stone and enlarged it to a slightly smaller size than the tunnels within. He kept the round shape, and added some rock formations around the entrance for visual effect. A slight tug and he had water droplets falling down the stalagmites onto the floor.

Taking a step back, Doc couldn't help but be proud of himself. His dungeon was actually located below a small hill near a forest and grass plain, and the entrance was perfectly angled to be visible from the forest and most of the plain. The earlier explosion added to the appeal, creating an uneven landscape leading up to his door.

Pleased, he returned to his room and informed Claire. She sighed and relaxed into the large slime, "It's done then; our first dungeon and my home." She giggled and rolled around on the slime's head, hugging herself happily.

"Doc, do you think Mommy would be proud of me?" She asked him tentatively.

Doc smiled at her, "Of course, Claire, you did a good job helping me; even if you pushed me to the brink of annoyance."

Claire giggled some more, "I was channeling 'my inner Mommy.' I couldn't do it as well as her, though."

Doc sent a silent prayer toward whatever dungeon had Claire's mom as his or her partner. "Now what, Claire?"

She pointed down, "Now it's the rest of your life. Expanding, evolving, learning, deepening; everything is left for you to do now. For now, why don't you practice using your boss in battle?"

"Okay, then," Doc said as he slid back into his slime body. Feeling cheeky, he formed tentacles and wrapped them around Claire's body, tickling her. She screamed in giggles and struggled to escape his slimy grip. He chased her the rest of the day as a slime and actually managed to fall asleep with her in his new body.

***

The two of them had two days of practice before Doc sensed something approaching. In happy expectation, the two of them spied out to see who was coming toward them. Doc had made a tiny tunnel for Claire to use to navigate the dungeon without being in the open. She stared out the peephole he made in the entrance as a group approached.

"Those four-legged beasts are called horses," she informed Doc, "They are simple beasts used to carry a rider over vast distances. I think those are human riders on their backs."

Doc had never seen another being beside Claire and slimes, and stared on in eager interest. The humans were dressed in brown material and had coverings on their heads.

"That's called leather armor. It is made from the skins of beasts," Claire told him, "I'd say this is a group of rangers, who specialize in exploration, information, and the forest."

"What kind of weapons do they have?" Doc asked eagerly.

Claire squinted, "I see bows and swords, so I don't think we have to worry about magic yet. Oh! That one is an elf!"

The elf looked a lot like the humans, but he had pointed ears, long white hair, and was taller than the others. He seemed to be leading the human rangers toward them from the forest line.

"Do elves have magic?"

"Yes, but unless they are mages, wizards, or sorcerers I wouldn't worry about it. No, I won't explain the differences now so don't ask; I can hear them now."

From what Claire could hear, the elf was leading the human rangers to the site of a loud noise days ago. From the sound of it, the humans had just returned from exploring and were tired from their previous trip. Something called a guild had ordered them to investigate before resting.

"That's the Adventurers' Guild they're talking about." Claire explained, "It's a group who manages adventurers to do things, like dungeon diving. From the sound of it, there is a human city nearby and an elf village that's closer to us. It seems the two villages have a good relationship."

The group arrived at the dungeon's entrance shortly after and dismounted from their horses. They approached the entrance cautiously with weapons drawn. Doc was experiencing fear, excitement, and eagerness all at the same time as they approached.

"This wasn't here a few days ago," the Elf said in a foreign language.

The human who was in the lead eyed the entrance and said, "It is most certainly a new dungeon, and well worth the rush we put in to get here."

Doc didn't understand them, but Claire translated for him.

The human nodded and turned his attention to his men, "Men, it's our job to evaluate this dungeon for the Adventurers' Guild to rate. Are you ready for some action?"

The cheers obviously meant the men were excited. Doc cheered too, but only Claire heard him. She giggled.

The elf's head shot around to stare at the peephole. Claire stumbled back in surprise.

"It seems someone is watching us," He informed the human leader, "And is quite pleased by our presence."

"Well, that just makes it more interesting." The leader grinned at the elf, "Come on now, men, and let's see what perils await." The elf, the human leader, and eight men entered the dungeon.

"Claire, it doesn't seem like they are scared, is that good?" Doc asked.

Claire shook her head, "No, unfortunately. It means they aren't taking us seriously and will try to take your crystal."

Doc frowned, "How do we change that?"

Claire smiled evilly, "Oh, all we have to do is scare them. What fun this will be!" Doc noted that dungeon pixies loved a good prank as much as their brethren.

The group entered and walked down the tunnel into the first room. The elf was frowning as they finished inspecting the room and found nothing.

"Must be a newborn to not have any traps," he said.

The human leader laughed and clapped his hand onto the elf's back, "That just means easy money, don't worry so much."

The elf frowned at him, "I don't take pleasure in killing newborns, especially for profit."

The leader sighed, "Would you prefer we left all dungeons alone? You know the risk."

"True, but I still don't like it." The elf sighed, twisting his sword.

The group made its way into the second tunnel. By pure luck, they missed the two pitfall traps and successfully entered the second room. As the last man entered, the ceiling slimes began their drop onto the men.

"Slimes!" The leader cried out, and the room broke into chaos. Slimes were easy to kill, but in a panic without any magic the men threw out any form of rational thought. One man had a slime land directly on his face, and was running around screaming as it fed on his hair. Another was forced to abandon his weapon as another slime chewed on it. One man even ran screaming back down the tunnel to the surface.

The elf and the leader remained calm as they fought the slimes.

"Calm down!" The leader shouted, "Aim for the cores you fools, the cores!"

The leader, wielding a long sword and a dagger, swung around and sliced the slime in half that was on the man's head. It dissolved quickly as the core fell to the floor. The elf swung with mesmerizing grace as he sliced the air itself with his weapon. Out of the nine men in the room, only five had been directly hit by the slimes. The little monsters moved slowly on the floor and were easy targets once everyone calmed down. They used their knives, swords, and axes to hit the cores and exterminate the slimes.

Fifteen slimes perished in the room. At that moment, all the men bent over to catch their breath. The leader remained standing, showing no indication of fatigue.

"I didn't expect slimes in this dungeon; an unfortunate mistake on our part." The leader lamented as he straightened his back, "I've never encountered a slime dungeon before. Hell, it's not often we fight slimes in the first place." He eyed the corridor beyond, "I'm not too keen on going any further without magical assistance," he added.

The elf nodded, "Indeed, wise decision, Sir Kenneth. Your role was merely to observe and report, not to conquer."

The leader, named Sir Kenneth, gave the elf an angry glare, "I told you it's Ken, not Kenneth. Who do you think you're talking to, elf?"

The elf held up placating hands, "My apologies," and he added, "Are you not a man short?"

Ken eyed his men and barked out, "Where's Perkins?"

The men muttered among themselves before one of them pointed to the corridor that led to the surface. Deciding the dungeon was too much for them right now, the group turned and left the dungeon, but not before coming across the pitfall trap Perkins had fallen into. Ken shook his head as he peered in, watching the last of Perkins' equipment being eaten by the slimes.

"Damned fool, running away from a fight in a dungeon. At least he was single, I hate delivering bad news to families." He made a gesture toward the pit, and then they left the dungeon. Doc and Claire watched them remount their horses and leave before they released their breaths.

From the slime boss, Claire smiled up at Doc, "Congratulations! You have survived your first dungeon dive. You even claimed a life! Few dungeons can claim taking a life on their first experience."

Doc winced, "Is killing really something to be proud of? I kind of feel like I should have let him escape, or at least kept him alive somehow."

Claire shook her head, "You had to show them you meant business in order survive, Doc. Dungeon diving is a risk all adventurers experience in order to become rich. There is no risk without reward, you know? They claimed the fifteen cores from the slimes they killed, and you claimed their foolish friend. By the way, you should have gotten a boost of power from that death."

Doc nodded, "Yeah, I got some stuff in my astral bag and some mana. The loot I got from him seems different from what he had on before."

Claire nodded, "Items you take are changed by your mana, however, powerful things, such as heavily enchanted weapons, are not changed when you absorb them. Sometimes items with strong emotional feelings can also be unaffected, but for the most part, the loot gets transformed into a generic form. All in all, a good first experience if I do say so myself."

She yawned and stretched her arms back, "Now, it's time for us to rest, and then you'll be back to work to improve your dungeon."

"Yes, dear."

Claire blushed, "Stop it! That's embarrassing!"

Doc chuckled and then moved into his boss' body for a good night sleep with his partner.

Chapter 5

While Doc and Claire rested from their first dungeon dive, the group of rangers, led by Sir Kenneth, third son of the ruler of Duran, returned to their city. About a day's ride away, the human city of Duran was one of the crowning jewels of the land. Duran sat in the western plain of the kingdom, next to a large forest where a small elves community was located. Leo was the elf who was part of Sir Kenneth's ranger group. He was an Elvin elder guardian. He and Sir Kenneth had worked together before and had become good friends.

Doc's dungeon was located near these two places, and unlike other kingdoms in the world, they were made up of independent city states which competed against each other, but worked together when they felt threatened by invaders. The city of Duran and the elves village worked together and traded so much that racial issues were a rare problem, and when it occurred, it usually came from outsiders.

The ranger group rode through the gates of Duran and down the center street to the castle. Ken was in a hurry to report to his father and the elves representatives so his men could rest. They had returned from the scouting mission organized to investigate the noise they had heard coming from the plains and, being a caring leader, he knew that his men were exhausted and needed rest.

The rangers were veterans of many battles; however, they were all fatigued from their journey and especially from the dungeon battle where they lost one of their own. Even as they rode their horses down the street, Ken could see their weariness and depression.

Leo rode up beside him, "Ken, I am sorry about Perkins."

Ken sighed, shaking his head, "Don't bother, you tried to stop us from going in the first place. I just wanted to give my men a little reward for their troubles, but I guess that was too greedy."

Leo patted Ken's back, a human gesture he wasn't quite comfortable with which brought a smile to Ken's face. "Yeah, you're right. All that is left to do is report back to the king."

Leo sighed and shook his head, patting his horse, "You know, he wants you to call him 'Father,' right? You break his heart every time you call him 'King.'"

Ken laughed, "He's a sly one to fool you elves. True, it bothers him, but he just exaggerates it for the sake of appearance. I'll call him 'Father' when those petty nobles aren't around. You know that the third son has no chance to inherit, so why make a scene out of family right?"

Leo sighed, "I'll never understand you humans, but whatever makes you happy."

They rode on in silence up to the castle gates. Duran was a round-shaped city, a common shape in the plains. A large wall surrounded the city and an inner wall protected the castle in the middle of the city. It served as a second siege wall in case of attacks, and was just as impressive. The castle itself was more of a large manor house than a fancy stone castle, mostly due to the lack of material in the area needed to build its walls.

The rangers dismounted inside the gate and gave their horses to the stable master, who nodded at them.

"Ye father awaits in his throne room with ye Elvin folk. They be knowin ye coming."

Thanking him, Ken and Leo led the rangers up the stairs to the large ornate oak doors. Nodding at the guards, Ken opened the door and walked in. The throne room was like the castle itself; practical and functional to relate to the common people. A large fireplace sat in the center of the room, used for cold nights and great feasts. Rooms and corridors ran out from every wall, and a simple wooden throne sat in the back with fancy chairs beside it.

King Duran sat in the throne with a smile on his face as the rangers approached. As king, he inherited the name of Duran on the day of his ascension to the throne, to show the connection of king to city. His beautiful wife Queen Nia sat in a smaller throne beside him, also smiling at the return of their son.

To their left, the elvish representatives sat in trees that they had grown in the shape of chairs. Ken recognized them as elders, but knew nothing of their names or their views. To the King's right sat the minister of the church and the head of the noble table: Father Tobias and Lord Mannis. Father Tobias, while not a leader in the church of light, was an honest man who represented the church in Duran. He was a kind faced man who had lived for many years and was well known for his teachings in the chapel. Lord Mannis was, to Ken, a perfect example of a typical noble: he was selfish, arrogant, cunning, wise, and loyal. The man was known to never let others do work for him, yet somehow always knew things he wasn't privy too. Ken always felt a strange mix of fear and admiration whenever he looked at the man.

While the other men kneeled, Ken and Leo bowed to the authority. King Duran arose.

"Welcome Ranger Commander Kenneth and Master Elf Leo. You are welcome in theses halls."

At that, the two straightened up and relaxed. The king smiled and called for chairs for the two. Once the servants brought two simple chairs, the other men were dismissed and left the throne room.

King Duran stretched and nodded to the two of them, "Well, now that the boring items are done, why don't you report what you encountered, Sir Ken? I couldn't help but notice you were one man short."

Sir Ken nodded, "Reporting sire: After a day's ride, we came across a hill near the forest. From the surrounding stone and dirt, the explosion came from a cave entrance in the hill, and judging by the amount of refuse, the entrance had been much smaller when the explosion occurred."

He explained how they entered the suspected dungeon and the battle that had followed, finishing with the death of Perkins and their subsequent return. The king frowned and looked thoughtful at the news.

"I know losing one of your men was hard, so accept my condolences. Was he with family?"

Ken shook his head, "No, sir. He was alone and lived in the ranger house."

King Duran sighed, "Well, at least you won't have to deliver the news. Master Leo, do you agree with Sir Ken's report?"

Leo nodded, "Indeed, King Duran. What Ken reported was all true. If I may add, we were listened to at the entrance and I heard a quiet giggle."

Lord Mannis leaned forward with a small smile, "Would you say it was a dungeon fairy, perhaps?"

"Possibly sir, but my eyes saw nothing my ears could hear."

Lord Mannis nodded and leaned back, turning his head toward the king. "My king, if this is indeed a new dungeon, it could be a profitable venture for us; especially with these slime cores." He gestured at the 15 slime cores Sir Ken had displayed while giving his report, "These cores can be made into healing potions that would create a new enterprise for our city. I see great wealth if we play this right."

King Duran nodded and turned to Father Tobias, "Father, what is the church's view on this new dungeon?"

Father Tobias leaned back into his chair; he looked thoughtful. "Well, the church is neutral on the matter of slimes unless they become too destructive. If the dungeon held undead or demons, I believe our gods of light would have sent us a sign to purify it. As it stands, the church could make use of healing potions to assist in our healing efforts. Clerics are hard pressed to cure all the problems and few are choosing a life in the church."

"How about your feelings Master Elves?" King Duran asked the representatives.

One of the elders stood and regarded the humans. "We live with nature, and as long as the dungeon does not harm the area, we are also neutral in regards to its existence. However, we should deliberate over the rights to it."

Lord Mannis raised an eyebrow and grinned, "My dear elder, I would be happy to accept the responsibilities of the dungeon.

The elder inclined his head toward Lord Mannis with a small smile of his own, "We wouldn't want to trouble you with such a trivial matter, Lord Mannis."

The king coughed and nodded to the two in front of him, "You two are dismissed, no need to listen to politics. Sir Kenneth, give your final report to the scribe when you get the chance and take the rest of the day off."

Grateful, Ken and Leo bowed and quickly exited the room while voices had begun to rise. Ken closed the door and sighed. "Well, looks like we'll have some work to do once they hash it out in there."

Leo was faintly amused, "I'm sure. If you need me, I'll be at the Elvin Embassy." They bowed to each other, and Ken watched Leo's disappearing form. He was startled from his thoughts by a tackle that almost knocked him over. He turned to find his younger sister hugging him tightly.

"Welcome back Ken!" Princess Diana cried out. The princess and her younger twin sister Hilda had recently come of age and were well regarded as the beautiful twins of the city. While Hilda preferred court matters and politics, Diana found her calling with the sword. She had trained with most branches of the army and guard, and would soon join Ken as a temporary ranger.

Ken sighed and rubbed her head affectionately, "Dear sister, what would mother say if she saw you jump random men?"

She stuck her tongue out at him, "Mother has long since given up on me and dotes on Hilda now. Her hope is that I'll meet a dashing general and settle down with him and bare his offspring. Load of rubbish in my opinion anyway." She smiled up at him.

Ken chuckled and tickled her, "Good luck with that plan; any officer knows they'd have to fight through me for your hand."

Diana giggled and escaped his clutches. She was dressed in full ranger gear, with her black hair wrapped into a braid down the side of her head. A pair of daggers lined belt and a bow hung off her back. "When can I ride to the ranger house with you, brother?"

Ken waved her off, "Come off it girl, I've just returned from battle and need a warm bath and soft bed. Ask me later."

Diana stared up with wide, excited eyes, "Is it true what they say, that a new dungeon was come to being? Was it as cool and dangerous as they say?"

Ken shrugged, "I've never heard of a dungeon described as "cool" before, unless it's a northern dungeon. It was a simple dungeon with slimes, and it cost me the life of one of my men."

She drooped at the news, "I'm sorry Ken."

He smiled and hugged her, "The cost of command little one; someday you'll understand it for yourself. Now, off with you. I need my rest."

She nodded and ran off, pausing before a corner to ask, "Do you think we'll be assigned to look at it again?"

"Most likely father will send us to secure the area once the politics are completed. If you're good, I may consider bringing you along."

She winked and disappeared around the corner. Ken sighed and scratched his head. He really wanted that bath now for his sister had wrapped him in her own sweaty attire.

Chapter 6

Doc and Claire began to work on replenishing their dungeon after a well-deserved long rest. As it turned out, the human's death had increased Doc's capacity to hold mana; even if it was just a tiny drop in a large well.

Doc felt a sense of trepidation about this discovery. "Does growing stronger really require the deaths of many adventurers? I'm not sure how I feel about that."

Claire sighed, but she smiled up at him. Doc had been mulling over the human's death ever since they woke up. While he accepted that the death had been necessary to prove a point, he was very obvious in his attitude toward killing. It refreshed and relaxed her, because it meant he would never endanger the two of them by killing on purpose.

"In all honesty, you don't have to kill to gain power; killing is one of the many methods that could increase your capacity. The easiest way would be to actively spread your influence everywhere, but that would corrupt the area and spawn dangerous monsters born from your power on the surface. Those types of dungeons are known as Corruption Dungeons, and are the most dangerous of your kind. They are always targeted once found, and rarely survive past their first year. On the other hand, your powers would slowly increase over time without doing anything, but that would be rather boring. Having living things die within your dungeon is a middle ground between being benign and being too dangerous to be allowed to live. Just set up your dungeon traps, and then the fools will die in them. You get power, the adventurers don't have to deal with fools, and everyone wins."

Doc sighed, "Well, okay then, I guess that's the best solution. By the way, is there any way you can change your clothes? They look really uncomfortable on you."

Claire's transformation had completed in their sleep, and she was a pleasantly busty pixie girl now. Unfortunately, her previous outfit had been designed for her previously gender neutral form, and thus was now actively trying to kill her.

Claire looked down and frowned, "I need my house for that, so I guess this is as good a time as any to make it." She flew up to her pedestal and pointed to Doc, "Now Doc, I'm going to begin making my house, which means I'll be moving some of your inner wall around to make room. No peeking is allowed until I am done, and afterwards you cannot enter without permission. If you do, mommy taught me suitable ways to make you regret your decision. If you have a question, ask away and I'll help you, but don't do anything new without my consent."

Doc rolled his crystal light across the ceiling, "Whatever you say dear."

Blushing with a pout on her face, Claire pointed at the pedestal wall and created a door. She walked over, opened it, stepped through, and closed it behind her. Doc felt her forming a tunnel, but moved his attention back to the dungeon.

He had remade his slimes and brought the total number up to 100. The floors were often times completely covered in little slimes, and one of the pitfall traps had already been accidentally triggered by a mass of slimes. Yes, Doc had decided to call a group of slimes a "mass."

"Claire, can I create new rooms?" He asked her.

"Yup. Within your dungeon, you are in complete control. You cannot shrink or grow the space available to you, but the entire dungeon territory is movable under you power. For instance, you can make stairs and move the rooms above you or below you. Spreading your influence in the ground will increase your territory, and thus the available room you have to work with. However, your heart room and my house will always be together."

"Good to know." Doc thought to her, "Not that I have considered it before."

"Meanie." He got this the subtle feeling that she was sticking her tongue out at him.

Smiling, Doc focused on his dungeon. The three existing rooms were not enough for his taste or protection, and he wanted more. Originally, he had to carve his way through the stone in order to spread his influence and expand his territory. Now, he could actively spread his magic through the earth that existed next to his walls.

Focusing on that, he spent the rest of the day changing the surrounding earth to fulfill his needs. As it turned out, Doc found that he couldn't spread his influence beyond a certain area. His territory projected itself outward in a spherical form, so the area he could use to create his dungeon was about average in height, length, and width. According to Claire, a dungeon could shape its territory into any form as long as the actual area stayed the same.

Once his influence reached its limit, Doc went ahead and began shifting himself around. He moved his room to the bottom of his influence and created an additional floor to separate the entrance. His dungeon was now starting to look like a "real one."

The first floor held the entrance with the three original rooms, but now the third room held a staircase down to the second floor. It was also a pitfall room with a single path through it where the wrong step would lead to slimes. The second room was still the ambush room, and pitfall traps had been added to the entrance corridor. The second floor held 4 more rooms that were in a counter clockwise rotation that led to his room. The traps were intermingled as well, with a new addition Doc came up with. He created many holes in the ceiling that would be impossible to avoid and had slimes climb into some of them. This would force adventurers to look up, risking a pitfall trap or air ambush.

Satisfied with his work, he moved himself into his boss body to inspect it. He had discovered earlier that he could read information about creatures by using magic to form the blue screen. He already had practiced by observing both the regular slimes and his personal slime.

Slimes are small gelatinous masses capable of devouring anything by absorbing them into their bodies. Lacking in intelligence and wisdom, they rely on their instincts and luck to find prey. Their cores are useful in potions and their bodies can be used to create certain poisons. His slimes had a general magic attribute, meaning it had no strengths or weaknesses when facing other forms of magic. Because the slimes were created in a dungeon, they were all connected to his hive consciousness. Due to their lack of intelligence, they would not understand his orders, but were capable of instinctively understanding what he needed them to do.

His personal slime was a different species altogether. It was an overslime; a slime that had accumulated power to grow to great size in comparison to the normal slimes. It had grown to a height equal to the waist of a grown man, and was much swifter than its smaller brethren, capable of launching its body short distances and forming small tentacles to wrap prey. It also had a general magic attribute and thus no inherent magic weakness or strength. Also, because it was his boss monster, it possessed a much higher agility than a normal overslime.

"I guess that means an overslime is normally a slightly stronger slime, but becoming a dungeon boss raised it to a much more dangerous level," Doc mused, "I wonder if I'll be able to evolve my slimes soon?"

"Drop that line of reasoning right now." Doc winced at Claire's sharp tone in his head.

"I was wondering where you were Claire; I guess that means your house is done?"

"It is, but don't change the subject. Evolving your monster requires a lot more experience and power than you currently have, so give up on it for now," she cautioned. "Instead, let's check each other's work."

She opened her door and flew out into the dungeon. In turn, Doc moved his awareness into her house to see what she had done. Doc had never seen a "house" before, but he assumed she meant living quarters and wasn't surprised by what he saw.

Claire had formed tiny rooms for herself in the back wall. It was complete with a room for sleep, a room to sit, and a room where he assumed she ate food. He had never seen her eat food besides mana, but that didn't mean she couldn't. He also took the responsibility to fully appreciate her new outfit.

She now wore a tiny purple dress with a graceful neckline and a longer petal skirt complete with purple stone earrings. Her dress was covered in silver lines that swirled up and down her body. Her luscious brown hair flowed down her back in waves and sparkled with purple stone ornaments.

"I like your outfit, but what's with all the purple?" He asked.

He heard her giggle as she flew through the tunnels, "It's because you're purple, you goof! Your stone was all I had to work with. Does it suit me?" He sensed her focus on his response.

"Well, I can't compare since you're the only female I know, but I'd say you look fine."

Somehow, he sensed a bit of disappointment from her, but it was quickly lost in her excitement. "Wow, Doc! You really did a great job! I love the new ceiling traps and this floor path!"

"Glad you like it." He smiled, "Is there anything else I can do?"

"Not really, sadly enough. You've done everything you could with the power you have, so now it's time for the waiting game; which is the worst part of being a dungeon."

Doc sighed, "Can I spend it sleeping?"

"Not all of it, but go ahead and sleep now. I'm going to go get some things for my house," Claire added.

Doc was instantly alert, "Do you mean outside? Isn't that dangerous for you? I can't help you if anything goes wrong out there."

He sensed her dismissal, "Don't worry about it. I just want some leaves. I'll be right back, okay?" She flew out the dungeon entrance before he could stop her. Fretting, Doc moved all his awareness to his entrance and watched her small form enter the forest. He didn't feel safe until she returned with a bundle of plants in her arms.

"Please don't do that again Claire, what if someone caught you?" He begged her.

"I understand your worry Doc, but I wanted to get some plants before it became impossible to leave. Here, why don't you use this plant I got for you?" She took the plant, complete with roots and leaves, and sat it on the floor. Doc eyed the tiny sprout.

"What is it?"

"That is an herb plant, I think. Since your slimes are good for potions, I figured growing this plant inside you will increase your reputation as a dungeon where a lot of healing components can be found."

Doc was skeptical, "I thought I couldn't control living things."

Claire nodded, "You are correct, but plants are a unique addition that can adapt easily in dungeons. When in a dungeon, plants gain the ability to feed off the mana that permeates your walls instead of the sun. They also spread quickly so long as the surface they grow on holds your mana. You can remove your mana from parts of your surfaces as well, which will limit the growth of the plants if you so choose. Your slimes can feed on them as well, so feel free to experiment with them for a natural evolution."

"What is a natural evolution?"

"Sorry," said Claire. "I forgot you don't know about that yet. Natural evolution occurs in nature, when a monster satisfies certain criteria to evolve on their own into a stronger monster. Dungeons can cause evolution to occur by using their mana to compensate for the criteria, but like metals, you can only create what you are familiar with. For instance, you would not be able to create a gelatinous slime because you don't know what it looks like. On a more important note the stronger the evolution, the more mana it requires. When you force a slime to evolve, the process will continue to completion even if you wish it to stop. If you use too much mana, you will drain yourself to death. Many newborn dungeons have accidentally killed themselves by going too fast from this, so be careful."

"Gotcha!" Exclaimed Doc, "By the way, I think that plant is growing already."

Indeed, the herb had already taken root on his floor and was beginning to grow. Claire clapped her hands in happiness.

"Great! Now your room will be covered in beautiful plants in a day or two."

Doc paused a moment, thinking about what she had just said. "Your old home didn't have plants because of the dungeon type right?"

Claire drooped, "Yup, because the zombies rotted everything. Dungeon Pixies spend most of their life underground, and it is in our nature to love being near plants. Mommy kept some potted plants in her house away from the zombies; plants she had managed to bring in before the zombies were prevalent. I always told myself I'd have plants in my dungeon."

"Your dungeon?"

She giggled, "Our dungeon. Now, don't let the plants spread out of this room. We want to make these plants the dungeon reward for beating the boss. They will also serve to hide your body and my house."

"Yes, dear."

"Stop that!" Claire commanded.

Chapter 7

As it turned out, Claire was right about the wait. Doc had never been so bored in his single month of existence. He sighed again as he watched the slimes bump into each other. It had gotten so boring that they had started betting leaves on which slime would be able to get by the overslime and reach the back wall.

"Slime A is heading toward the goal, will he succeed?" He commented monotonously.

Claire glanced over from the overslime's top, "I'll bet two leaves on failure."

Slime A was heading toward the back wall, but barely grazed the overslime and wobbled away. Claire and Doc sighed together at the sight. "That makes 50 failures to get past the overslime; and I owe you 100 leaves," Doc lamented.

Claire groaned and rolled over, setting a pair of small twigs down she had been using to 'knit,' as she called it. "I don't even want any leaves. Can't we bet some of the gold you've been making? How about the silver or copper? I'll even take iron at this point."

"You know better Claire, that's all for the adventurers when they get here," Doc scolded. Since filling out into his full dungeon territory, Doc had come across a small silver vein and learned its properties. Finding the silver had completed, according to Claire, his list of metals used to create coinage for the adventurers. Doc decided to form copper and silver coins for the astral bag slime drops, but kept the mining area limited to copper.

"[Sigh]... But I want to make some pretty things for my house," she pined, "I want some shiny things!"

Doc chuckled, "Well, let's see what the adventurers bring in. I'll let you keep some shiny things from them, okay?"

This brightened her up immediately and she flew around the room in happiness, "Yay! Thank you,

Doc!" She blew him some kisses as she bounced on the overslime's head. He rolled his eyes and focused on his slimes.

His slimes were now up to 120, and spread evenly around his dungeon. The pitfalls held six, the skyfalls held three, and the rest of them were moving or hiding as puddles. All in all, a good basic dungeon set-up in his opinion.

The two were startled by a vibration in the earth. "What's that?" Doc asked excitedly. Claire flew up into her personal path to the peephole at the entrance.

"It's people!" She cried out happily, "I see a lot of adventurers and wagons. That means they are going to set up a base camp, and send people in to fight us."

The two of them happily watched as horse-pulled wagons and men came towards them carrying materials and equipment. They stopped before the first line of refuse from the explosion and began to set up things.

"Claire, what are they building?" He asked as they watched the men work.

"They are making houses, tents, and a shop," she informed him, "The houses and tents are to sleep in, and the shop is for selling the loot they get from us. Oh! I think I see some blacksmith equipment too; which means they expect some mining and tool repairs will be needed."

"Should I set up the mining areas now?" Doc asked.

Claire thought a moment, "Why don't you create a copper vein in the first room. You should replenish the copper when adventurers leave, and I advise you don't focus on that room when they are mining; it'll be very annoying otherwise."

Doc split his attention between growing the copper into veins and watching the men outside. He was fascinated by the humans; they were so interesting. They didn't have magic to make their homes, but they could use their arms and legs to make anything they needed. They were fast too; Doc could see a lot of small tents set up already.

"Do you think the elves will come too?"

"If they do come, it'll be later, after the humans are done. Oh, get ready for the scouts!" Claire shrieked excitedly. A small party was approaching the entrance; five men in full metal armor and wielding some very shiny swords. Doc could see the glow around the swords that indicated magic.

"Those must be strong adventurers," Doc thought to himself, "I wonder if they want to take my crystal." Doc kind of doubted it though, because of all the work the humans were doing to make places to sleep. "No matter, I want to see what they can do."

The two occupants watched the men enter the dungeon without hesitation; strolling right in with their weapons drawn. Inside, water drops plopped down from the ceiling, forming puddles on the floor. It was a cool effect Doc had designed to hide the slime puddles. The men did not even pause at the sight, and began swinging their swords at every puddle in their path. Doc winced as his slime army disappeared rapidly. "Claire, I think those men have dealt with slimes before."

Claire was following the men from her path and watching them with Doc. "Those look like ranked B adventurers; very strong adventurers who are good at scouting out dungeons; it seems as if they have reached the first room."

The men entered the room after first observing the ceiling and walls. They moved slowly across the floor, testing each step for pitfalls. One of the men paused beside a wall and took out a small tool. He chipped at the wall and inspected it closely. He called over the others, and they grouped together and whispered to each other.

"They aren't whispering Doc; you just can't hear them because you're avoiding the room," Claire retorted, "Anyway, they're excited to find the copper vein."

The men exited the room, but not before the first man drew out a stick and pointed it down the hall. Instantly, a blue light shot down and illuminated all the pitfall traps in a blue light. Doc felt a little cheated as he watched the men easily avoid his traps. They even avoided the second room ambush by throwing stones into the room. The slimes fell harmlessly to the floor and were easily slain. They repeated the trick on the next corridor and entered the third room.

"This should be new to them, so maybe I can trick one!" He thought happily to himself. Doc didn't expect a strong man to die, but watching someone fall into a pitfall was funny and entertaining. The adventurers repeated their earlier tactic, spreading out and checking the floor as they slowly moved forward. Unfortunately for them, the pitfalls were a little thicker in this room, and 2 of the men fell into pitfalls after thinking the floor was safe. Claire and Doc laughed as they watched the two men rolling around the slimes and sputtering curses. The slimes were having trouble eating the armor, but had some success slipping inside the cracks. They didn't get too far when the leader blasted both holes with fire and evaporated all the slimes.

"That one must be a warrior mage," Claire observed, "He's currently making fun of the two that fell in." Indeed, while they helped the men up, they were greeted by laughter and back clapping. The mage adventurer pulled the stick thing out again and illuminated the proper path as they all walked out of the room and down the stairs. The same thing happened for the rest of the dungeon, and now the five men were standing at the front of the boss room.

The herb plants had grown quickly along the walls and ceiling, but were eaten off the floor by the slimes. The effect was a dimly purple illuminated room with plants growing everywhere except the floor with one large slime in the middle of the room.

"Okay, now it's my turn!" Doc tensed up as he flowed into his slime boss body. He jiggled as the men entered and took stances facing him, eager to experience his first fight. "Attack!" He cried out in his head, launching himself at the man on the far right.

The men were startled for half a second, not expecting a dungeon boss to make the first move. It was brief, but enough for Doc to almost reach the man. He threw out his tentacles and wrapped them around the waist and sword.

The man began yelling and struggling, but was stuck by the purple tentacles. Doc picked the man up and stuck him on his head, impaling the man up to his waist in slime. He also ate the sword. The captured man struggled lamely on top of Doc's head, trying everything to escape, but couldn't find a solid enough surface to push against.

The other men moved quickly and began their attack. The mage stayed in the back and began firing fireballs at Doc. The other three ran at him and swung their swords. Doc dodged a fireball, then slapped at the swords with his tentacles. He pushed one of the men away as he desperately tried to avoid being sliced by the swords. As the third man recovered, the other slashed high and low at Doc, cutting one of his tentacles off.

Annoyed, Doc prepared another lunge. As he prepared to jump, the man in him cried out a warning. Instantly, the sword wielders dived out of the way as Doc surged forward. He missed, and ended up surrounded by the remaining warriors. A burning pain let him know that the third man had pierced him from behind. As Doc turned his attention, the mage burned him from the front with fireballs.

It was a route after that for the men, with Doc unable to split his attention between the four combatants. With a silent gurgle, he felt his dungeon boss die and dissolve. He moved back to the dungeon and sighed as he watched the overslime dissolve into a slightly bigger core, some silver, and a very embarrassed man. The adventurers were clapping and laughing and doing other forms of congratulations.

"Well, at least they had fun," Doc said with a small smile.

Claire sent him a questioning feeling from across the room, "Why did you not eat the man immediately? He would have given you a nice boost to your power and that armor would have been nice too."

Doc shook his crystal, figuratively, "I wanted them to understand that this dungeon isn't a threat, but I did want them to see I could have killed if I wanted to. Err, speaking of, are they aware of my existence?"

Claire was amused by the question, "Not in the sense that you are an individual. Most adventurers believe a dungeon is a hive mind made up of many monster minds. The idea of a single mind controlling everything is not a common one among the sentient races, though perhaps some of the smarter individuals suspect it."

They watched the men collect the loot and take some of the plants from the walls. "Hey Claire, how do they leave now? Do they walk back the way they came?"

"Watch," she told him.

The adventurers came together and disappeared in a flash of light. Doc was surprised, "Where did they go?"

"For small dungeons like you, adventurers can buy a magic talisman that allows them to leave whenever they are out of battle. When you get bigger, one of your possible powers will allow for areas to be connected by portal or teleporting glyphs. It's one of the cooler things a dungeon can make, like different realities for adventurers to travel through."

Doc didn't feel like asking about what she meant, but instead focused on the adventurers leaving the dungeon in high spirits. "I can't wait for more of them to come," he thought happily.

Chapter 8

Guild vice-leader Mary sighed as she gazed at the growing settlement in front of her. She heard second hand the report on the new dungeon from her leader, Guild Master Vance. This new turn of events intrigued her; she was very curious about this place so she decided to volunteer and lead the Adventurer Guild Outpost at the new dungeon outpost. She did not realize that the task would be a rather boring one at the start.

"Whew" she sighed out, "I guess I should have expected this, but I guess I was overly eager." She was currently sitting on a chair behind a small table in one of the bigger tents. This was the branch office for the guild until a more permanent structure was set up. She leaned over and let her head out of the tent to check out the dungeon's entrance, which was facing her direction. She was waiting for the return of the scout team that had set out earlier to inspect the dungeon.

She had nothing to do and no one to talk to until the team's arrival. The workers were too busy to speak to her, the elves would not be coming this season, and the other adventurers were back at Duran getting ready. Until they heard back from the scouting team, the dungeon's level was unknown, and therefore, off limits to all who would want to enter.

This wasn't Mary's first solo assignment, but it was her first time dealing with a dungeon. Dungeons were not common in the plains, as they preferred to form in areas with large amounts of stone. This dungeon seemed to be growing out of a small hill, an uncommon enough thing to find in the plain, and had its entrance lead deep under the ground. Mary was curious how the dungeon hive mind would adapt to the handicap of the plains. The fact that it was a slime dungeon only added to the mystery, as no slime dungeon had ever been recorded before.

Her thoughts were interrupted by cries and cheers from the camp. From her vantage point, she could see the five men returning from their trip in triumph, waving to the cheers of their fellow men. Mary rolled her eyes at the sight; she knew the men too well and felt happy to see them.

The B-ranked adventurer group was led by a battle mage named Koran Stakes, an ass of a man when it came to women; believing himself to be a gift unto them. To add to his arrogance, he also possessed noble blood. His father was an important figure in the city's Merchant Guild. The only reason she tolerated him was that he had the skill and strength to back up his boosts, and was very thorough in completing assignments. His men, who were sons of other minor nobility, always backed up his claims.

The men strolled over to her tent and closed the flap behind them for some privacy. Koran walked up to her wearing his trademark arrogant grin. "How about a date with the dungeon conqueror, Miss Mary?" He swaggered, winking at her face.

Mary rolled her eyes and sat up, "I already told you Koran, you're not my type. I have a few hundred years on you and no patience for younglings."

Koran's smile faltered a moment, then came back as smooth as ever, "Whatever you say my dearest Mary, I know I can't compete with the lines of men desiring your attention."

She narrowed her eyes at him, noting the slight jab at her. Many men shied away from her when they learned of her half elf blood, and many looked to her in disgust for her advanced age. Men had their pride, and none desired to be old and dying while she was youthful still. Unlike a true elf, however, she had aged some over the years to resemble a woman in her thirties, but still young. Koran relished in the challenge of bedding her, but had no desire to keep her afterwards. Rumors in the darker parts of the city whispered of the girls who went with him and never returned.

"Be that as it may, I'm sure you are here for something beyond wooing me?" She asked.

Koran winked and dumped a bag filled with slime cores onto the table. "Behold the spoils of victory!" He boasted.

Mary inspected the cores with a keen eye and magic glasses. The cores were from simple slimes, and were not distinguishable from each other. The magic element interested her a little, being that it was a very rare affinity to have. A dungeon this close to the forest or plain should have had an earth or wind affinity, yet this one was completely neutral. In terms of value, they were worth a little more than a regular core and would be useful in potion crafting.

"Eighty slime cores of equal value with sixty copper per core will earn you... forty eight silver pieces. Now, report your experience," she barked at him after setting her glasses down.

He nodded. "The dungeon is young, consisting of two floors with three rooms on top and five on the second level, including the boss room. Standard slimes traps are present including pitfalls, puddles, and skyfalls. The first room is devoid of traps, but holds copper veins suitable for mining in safety. The rooms alternate from ceiling drops to pitfall paths and the same applies to the corridors between them. The boss room held an overslime that came up to my waist and displayed greater battle prowess than a normal overslime; it even managed to capture one of my men."

Mary raised an eyebrow, "Yet, I see all four of your men here. Did you manage to free him before he was killed?"

Koran frowned. "That's the strange thing; the monster had him up to his waist, but didn't eat him at all except for his sword. I can only assume that the sword gave it so much trouble it couldn't eat anymore."

Mary doubted that. During the mercenary period of her life, she had witnessed a certain type of slime devour two men and their horses at the same time with no trouble at all; the slime even ate all of their magic equipment! She nodded at Koran for him to continue.

"Due to his situation, my man was able to warn us about it when it leaped, and we surrounded the monster and slayed it after. It is my belief that it was easier to defeat due to the lack of experience the dungeon possessed when it came to adventurers. I would rate it somewhere from a C to a lower B in terms of scale of difficulty. The boss room was filled with basic healing herbs, uncommon in the nearby forest, and covered the walls and ceiling effectively. The dungeon core itself was hidden; either in a hidden room or deep under the plants themselves."

He took out the copper and plant samples they had taken and gave them to her along with the overslime core. She put on her glasses and observed them each. The copper and plants held no magic, but would be useful in the crafting guilds. The slime core itself was just a larger and purer form of the basic slime cores from earlier.

"I will inform the crafting guilds of the copper and herb deposits, and I will send your report to the Adventurer Guild in Duran," she said. "You are dismissed Koran." She waved him off as she took out pen and paper.

Koran frowned at her, but bowed and left the tent without a word. Mary eyed the entrance flap and resumed her writing. "That man will be a problem eventually," she thought to herself. "I shudder to think what would happen if he gained more power." She feared he had hidden secrets that no one knew about. At the same time, she couldn't help but chuckle to herself, "Well, at least things will be interesting around here."

***

Diana grinned to herself as she rode her horse into the camp. "This is so exciting! I get to come here all by myself and it's all thanks to Hilda!" She thought to herself. The day before, she had been talking with her sister and mentioned the new dungeon to her as well as her desire to look into its possible secrets; this made her sister smile at her.

"Don't worry sis, I'll help you out with that," Hilda said before leaving the room. Later that day, Diana had received orders from the head ranger himself to carry messages to the budding camp in front of the dungeon. Excited and joyful, Diana had grabbed her fastest horse and rode out as soon as she read her orders.

"Silly Ken, he still thinks I'm a little girl in need of protection." She grinned as she entered the camp. She knew Ken had agreed to take her to the ranger base in order to keep her out of trouble. He'd leave her there in the hands of the ranger masters, and have all sorts of fun in the dungeon without her.

"Not on my watch, no sir. This is the opportunity of a lifetime, and I'm not going to miss it," she thought to herself.

She got off her horse and marched over to one of the larger tents and poked her head in. "Message for the adventurer Koran!" She announced brightly.

Inside, a group of men were taking off their armor as they turned to look at her. The handsome one in the back walked to her with a cute smile. "That would be me darling. Thank you for the letter." She blushed as she handed him her delivery and waited patiently as he read the letter. His grin grew when he finished and looked back up at her. "Care to join us on a dungeon raid tomorrow? We have to explore some in order to get a good idea of what we're dealing with."

Diana jumped up in excitement, "That would be great! When can we meet?"

"Meet us just before the sunrise at the entrance. Have a good night." He waved her off with a smile as she skipped away to find a tent.

"Hey boss, didn't we already explore the dungeon? Why are we going back?" Asked one of his friends. Koran turned and winked at him.

"We have a little job to do gents, one that will let us have a little fun as well." Instead of his normal smile, Koran had an evil grin that was soon shared by the four of his friends.

Chapter 9

Doc was happily making new slimes in his dungeon when he sensed something. It was still dark outside, but he felt the approach of some people to his entrance.

"Claire, wake up!" He sent to her sleeping form, "Someone is coming our way."

Claire mumbled and rolled around on her bed, a new addition to her room made from plants and slime.

"Claire!" Claire woke up with a yelp and flew into the ceiling, startled by his yell. She groaned and rubbed her nose in annoyance.

"What is it, Doc?"

"Someone's coming our way, and it's still dark out," Doc informed her. Claire raised an eyebrow and began flying to the entrance.

"I didn't think they'd show up so soon," she muttered to herself as she flew down her tunnel.

"They? Do you know who is coming?" Doc asked curiously.

"Not who specifically, but I can guess the reasons for the visit," she said honestly. Taking her spot at the peephole she asked him, "Have you remade your dungeon boss yet?"

"No, I was just making more slimes. Should I go ahead?"

"No, save it for now, you may need it for later," Claire advised while eyeing the approaching humans.

Confused, Doc obeyed and moved curiously to the entrance to watch. There were four men in leather armor at his entrance, waiting for something. He didn't recognize them, but their presence seemed familiar.

"…Protect her…" Doc thought he heard a voice in his head, but he couldn't hear it anymore. His attention returned to Claire as she began speaking.

"Those are the men who came with the mage yesterday," Claire clarified, "However, they are not wearing their magic armor and wield plain swords. They did not come here to conquer you again."

The two were alerted to a new presence running up to join the men. Doc recognized the human aspects, but this human was not like the others. "Claire, this human has lumpy things on her, like you," he exclaimed.

For some reason, Doc sensed he had somehow offended Claire. "Doc, those are breasts. They are found on females of most species and used to feed their young. They are not lumps."

"So does that mean you have children? How'd you make them?"

Doc felt a mental back slap from a blushing Claire, who cried out, "No, you idiot! I don't have kids! They are there for when we have children, and used to attract a mate."

"Weird thing to use to attract mates," Doc muttered under his breath. He went on to say to her, "So does that mean bigger is better? I think you have bigger ones even though she is larger than you."

Claire was feeling rather smug when she said, "Yes it does, and yes I am, thank you very much. Now, be quiet so I can listen in."

The two focused on the conversation that started when the girl arrived.

"Am I late? Did Sir Koran go without me?" The female asked.

"Don't worry ranger, Master Koran had other matters to tend to and you're on time. We won't be going far in today, but you came prepared for battle correct?" One of the men asked.

The girl nodded and showed off her weapons, "I'm all set! Thank you for bringing me with you on your dungeon excursion." She bowed to them.

The men waved it off, "Think nothing of it young one, we are happy to help our junior to gain experience. It's important to learn what's expected of you sooner rather than later. Follow us."

They entered the dungeon, leading the girl into its dark depths. Doc watched them closely, somehow not feeling as excited as he had the day before.

"Claire, somehow I don't feel comfortable," he told her.

She nodded, "I guess being an old soul makes you more aware of situations like these. Most dungeons wouldn't care at all."

"What do you mean?" asked Doc.

Claire sighed, "Not everyone is a good person in the world. Mommy showed me that when I was younger. Some evil people like to use dungeons to do things and get away from punishment. Don't interfere and watch them."

"…Save…" The soft voice disappeared as fast as he heard it, sending a shiver through Doc. Doc was unsure now, but relented and watched the men lead the girl deeper into the dungeon.

"Is this your first time in a dungeon Mrs. Ranger?" Asked one of the men.

She nodded, "That's right, I haven't seen a dungeon before. Is it supposed to be this easy?"

"Don't worry; it'll get worse the further we go in," he reassured her. "The way to the first room is clear of traps for now and the room has a nice copper vein to mine."

"Wow! They didn't teach me at the castle about copper veins in dungeons." The girl was so excited she must have said something interesting. Doc wasn't the only one to notice because the man began eyeing her differently and coughing.

"Are you alright, sir?" She asked concerned.

The man nodded, "Don't worry, it's an old injury. Why don't you go ahead to the first room while I rest a moment? Take Jack with you while the others watch me."

"Are you sure?" She asked while hearing splitting up sounds.

"Don't worry; it's safe till the second tunnel. Go, don't let me hold you back," said the man.

The girl still looked unsure, but her eagerness overcame her reservations. So she and one of the men went on ahead to the room. The girl inspected the walls in fascination and asked the man about mines in dungeons. Meanwhile, Doc noticed that the other three men were huddled together and were arguing.

"She's from the castle! No way am I following the plan now, that's too much attention." One of the men was saying in hushed whispers.

"You idiot! You knew she was important, what difference does it make now? We have our orders from Koran, and failure to him would get us killed." Another argued.

"Screw that! I hear traitors to the crown are given over to those bastard elves, and they say they know ways to keep a man alive in pain for decades," the other man said.

The first man snorted, "And you don't think Koran can't? Besides, no one knows that she's here with us. To everyone, the girl was overeager and entered the dungeon without help and died of a terrible death. Those slimes are real useful for stuff like that, you know, and we can even have some fun before getting rid of her."

"The dungeon, what if it attacks us while we're still inside it? We had to leave our stuff behind so no one would recognize us while Koran's men wore the armor and swords today. We could die in here!"

"Listen, we aren't traveling farther than the first room. We'll have some fun in there; then we'll toss her body down the corridor and let the slimes finish her off. No one will be the wiser."

The man grumbled, but nodded. "Fine, but I get first dips on her chastity. I like my women pure when they scream."

The other two men laughed and clapped the man on the back as they headed toward the first room. Doc was horrified.

"They are going to kill that girl, Claire! Why would they hurt each other?"

Claire sent him her sad feelings, "I told you there are bad people in the world. Those men are going to use her, then dump her and leave her to die. I've seen it before, and it will happen again."

"I... I don't like that!" Doc muttered, "I... I don't want to see her... hurt. She's going to be hurt... going to die..." Doc's mumbling began to fall into gibberish, which began to concern Claire.

"Protect her..." Another shiver shook Doc as he began to lose control over his emotions.

"Doc, are you okay? Speak to me!" Claire called out, but Doc couldn't hear her anymore. He was completely focused on the scene in the first room.

***

"Jack was telling me all about the copper veins! Thank you for guiding me!" The girl was happy and bowing her thanks to the men.

The lead man smiled, "Always happy to help. Now, we need to discuss payment."

The girl tilted her head, confused. "Payment? How much do you want?"

The man nodded to Jack, who was slowly walking up behind the girl with his sword out. "Oh, don't worry about it. Like I said, juniors need to be taught what to expect by their seniors." In a flash, Jack cut the leather binding the girl's weapons to her and broke her bow as they clattered to the ground. The girl jumped back in fright as she stared wide eyed at her weapons.

"What, what is going on?" She asked, fear creeping into her voice.

The men chuckled, "Oh, why we're just going to have some fun. Now be a good girl and come to us." Two of the men were blocking the exit tunnel as the other two closed in on her, her back to the tunnel leading further in.

"You can't do this! I'm a princess! My father will kill you for this!" She cried out, fear overcoming her training as the men closed in on her with weapons drawn.

"Silly girl, no one knows you're here. No one knows your name. No one will care that you're gone." Said the leader with an evil grin. "That letter told us exactly what to do with you. Now, since that letter came from the palace, I think you should realize exactly who ordered this."

The girl backed up slowly as her eyes darted back in forth, "N...no...no one wants me dead! Everyone likes me, and I haven't done anything wrong."

"Silly girl, it's your existence that's the problem. No one is going to save you, and when they realize you're gone, they will all forget about you. All you ever were was a burden, an eyesore, and an embarrassment to your name. Why, your own family wants you gone."

The girl's knees buckled, "No, that can't be. You're lying!"

The man removed something and showed it to her, "See here, this is the royal seal of your family, isn't it? It may not be signed, but only your family has access to the seal."

The girl's face fell into despair as she looked at the document, tears falling down her face as she understood her folly. "I, I won't be killed by this!"

With a quick motion, she drew a dagger out of her sleeve and sliced the flimsy thing in half as the man jumped back. He laughed and waved his sword in the air.

"Come on then girl, bring your fight! I like my girls feisty and defeated." He swung his sword at her, barely missing as she leaped backwards. Her face was in complete panic as she tried to get a hold of herself, but the trauma and fear were not leaving her. The two men swung their massive swords, and all she could do to dodge them was to leap back and lean sideways. The men didn't even give her a chance, one man's swing ending as the other's began. Her little dagger was worthless against their reach.

Seeing no way to run, she reared back and threw the dagger into the arm of the lead man, shouting

"I'd rather die than give you bastards what you want!" She turned and ran down the tunnel, leaving the man cursing in pain as he took the dagger out.

"Dammit! Get her Jack!" He shouted, prompting his partner to run after her into the tunnel.

Doc watched her run through his dungeon. He watched her sobbing and terrified while running toward his pitfall trap. He watched her fall, fall, and fall into his trap. The slimes came up to meet her. He could hear her anguished screams as she felt their gooey grip. He saw all of it, and could only watch in silence, a specter in the wind.

"Save her." He heard the voice a final time. And then, he just stopped thinking.

***

Hank growled as Lucas wrapped his arm with a piece of cloth. "Damn bitch, I'll treat her when Jack drags her back." He yanked his arm away from Lucas and looked at it. Blood was starting to seep through, but it was holding together. "Lucas, Mark, I get her pretty face first!" he barked at them. They nodded, unwilling to argue against him while he was furious.

They were interrupted by a loud scream, echoing down the tunnel.

"That that was Jack!" Lucas said, wide eyed.

Hank growled and got up, walking to the tunnel. "Jack, Jack, answer me!" He yelled down the tunnel. He heard no answer from the darkness. "Mark, go find him!"

Mark picked up a torch and lit it, heading down into the tunnel. He didn't get far before he ran back in fear. "It got him Hank, the slimes got 'em!"

Hank spat onto the floor and shook his head, "Damn idiot. I told him to be careful with the pitfalls."

"He ain't in no pitfall Hank, they be on top of him!" Mark cried out.

Before Hank could ask, they heard a rustling from the darkness. They turned to see a swarm of slimes slithering toward them from all surfaces.

"Run!" Hank cried, and the three of them bolted for the exit. They found the way blocked by another swarm of slimes, and found themselves trapped in the room.

"It wasn't like this before Hank; it wasn't like this at all!" Lucas wailed as they were surrounded.

"Shut up and light the torches, we can still get out!" Hank ordered. Quickly, each man held two torches and waved them at the slimes, creating a free space around them.

Hank laughed, "Ha! Stupid slimes are scared of fire! Let's go boys, slow and steady now." They never looked up to see a lone slime crawl right above them. They didn't see it begin to grow to a much larger size.

They did, however, feel it when it fell on them and smothered their fire.

And the slimes descended on their screams.

Chapter 10

Doc regained consciousness as Claire hit his crystal with her little fists. "Wake up Doc! Come on, you can't do this to me so soon!"

"Claire, is that you? What's going on?" He muttered, rousing himself and reconnecting with her mind. Claire sighed in relief and plopped back onto her table. "Thank goodness! I was really scared Doc!" She cried out and hugged herself.

"Why would you be scared? What happened?"

She sniffed and pulled her legs closer to her body, "You had a severe mental breakdown Doc. You lost your mind and became a force of destruction."

Doc was confused by her words, "What do you mean?"

"You lost your individuality," Claire explained, "You acted on your instincts instead of reason, as if you had fallen to the level of a newborn dungeon."

"I don't understand what happened; did someone hurt me?" He asked her with concern.

She shook her head, "No, but something set you off. I don't know why the girl made you like that, but you reacted badly to her situation."

The girl in his dungeon; he remembered her now. She was hurt and in danger. He had wanted to do something, but he couldn't remember. "Claire, what did I do?" He asked slowly.

"You killed them," she said simply, "You used all your power to kill the men and made sure they suffered for every bit of it. It was really scary because you didn't hear me at all. All that mattered was hurting them."

Doc shuddered, "That doesn't sound like me at all."

"I agree, but that's what happened. Did you know her?"

"What?" Asked Doc distractedly.

"The girl, did you know her?" Claire clarified, "She's the reason for your episode." Doc shook his head, "No, I've never seen her before. I just...didn't want her to die like that."

"That voice told me to save her. Was it because of it that I lost control?" He wondered to himself privately. He paused, "Did she die? I can't remember."

Claire hesitated, "Well, not exactly; but she isn't okay either." Claire pointed at the center of the room.

There, floating inside his overslime, was the girl. Her eyes were closed and her arms were down by her side as she floated peacefully within the slime.

Doc was floored, "What is this? What did I do?"

Claire floated down to the slime and sat on it, "Well, you saved her from being eaten, but I don't know if she's okay. It's been a few days since you 'saved' her, so she could be dead for all I know. I read the letter the men had on them, and she's some important person to the royal family in the human city."

"Royal family, is that the human leaders then?" He inquired.

Claire nodded, "Yes. Humans rule each other by birthright and ability. The king and his mate, the queen, are the leaders and their children are princes and princesses. The letter doesn't describe who she is, but I wouldn't be surprised if she was a princess herself."

Doc mulled this over in his head, "Can I release her?"

"I don't see why not," said Claire, "I'm curious to see if she's still alive or not. Let me hide first though." Claire flew over to her door hidden in the herbs and closed it behind her as she entered. "It's not in our interest to reveal our individual existences yet."

Doc shrugged, and moved his will into the overslime. The overslime jiggled, then slowly and carefully laid the girl out on the floor. She didn't move from her resting place. "Claire, is she dead?"

"How should I know?" She retorted, "You have to check her. Move to the floor and see if she's still breathing."

Feeling a bit foolish, Doc listened to the girl's body. She seemed to be breathing, and in fact, seemed to be getting faster breaths. Before Doc could ask what that meant, the girl slowly opened her eyes.

She slowly gazed around the room and locked onto the overslime. A small smile came over her tired face as she relaxed.

"I was saved by a slime. How silly, to be rescued when there is nothing else for me." She closed her eyes as tears began to flow down her face onto the floor. Feeling sad for some reason, Doc had the overslime form a tentacle to wipe away her tears.

The girl giggled at the touch, "Mr. Slime, are you saying it's okay for me to live? Will you take me in when no one else wants me?"

Slightly annoyed now, Doc had the slime slap the girl's face a few times with the tentacle, startling both the girl and Claire who was watching the scene.

"Doc, what are you doing? This is an emotional moment!"

"Her words annoyed me." He said defensively, "So I'm trying to wake her up."

"Don't slap her, you idiot!"

To their surprise, the girl began laughing in earnest. Her eyes were closed and she wasn't moving, but the girl's laughter filled the room. It mixed with her tears until she was a sobbing-coughing-laughing mess on the floor.

"Okay, Mr. Slime, I won't cry anymore. Is that what you want?"

Doc patted her with the tentacle.

The girl relaxed and her breathing started to slow down. "Okay, Mr. Slime. I won't cry anymore. I'll...be good. I... show my... thanks." She drifted off to sleep as a tiny light flowed from her body into the floor.

"She is your responsibility now..." Doc heard the voice more clearly this time, but he sensed it would no longer speak to him. He looked over toward Claire, "Claire, what did she give me?"

Claire was watching the girl, stunned. "Claire?"

She shook her head, "Something special for another day Doc. For now, let's get her out of the dungeon. I don't want the human adventurers blaming us for anything happening to her."

She flew out of her home holding a large thing to her chest. Doc recognized it as the thing the mean mad had had before.

"What are you doing Claire?" He asked.

She landed on the girl and stuffed the thing into her armor, "I'm making sure the humans focus on the letter instead of us. Let's carry her up to the entrance and leave her where they can find her."

Doc picked her up with his overslime and slowly carried her body through his dungeon up to the main entrance. His body couldn't go past his influence, but he could use his rapidly dissolving tentacles to deposit her gently by the entrance before returning to his room.

"Good job Doc. Now, with any luck they will begin searching for the traitor and the hero who saved the princess."

"What hero? Was there another human in the dungeon I didn't know about?"

Claire giggled, "Nope, I signed the letter on the back saying the dungeon explorer 'Doc' rescued her from her fate. They will search for a man while we get away without any trouble, and with a lot of gained power!" Doc watched her celebrating by bouncing on the overslime.

"You really are looking out for us aren't you?"

She smiled at him and rolled onto her belly, chin in her hands. "Of course, silly! You are my home, partner, and best friend, even if you are a silly fool interested in other women when you have me."

"What?" Said Doc.

She laughed, "I'm teasing you, silly. You wouldn't know the first thing about wanting a girl in the first place."

"I have a girl, you. Why would I want another?"

"You're sweet," she said, beaming at him, "Now, on a more important notice, we have more work to do! All those men were really strong and adding the sword you ate makes you a lot stronger. We need to upgrade your abilities now."

"How do we do that?"

"With the upgrade chart of course!" Claire waved her finger and the mana condensed into a familiar blue writing.

Ability	Description
Teleporting Glyph	Inscribe a glyph on every floor that allows adventurers to move from one floor to another easily. Must have cleared the floor to be able to move to it. Groups are restricted to the lowest level conquered by a member
Additional Race	Able to create an additional race to the one held. Increases dungeon diversity
Upgrade Monsters	Grants the ability to improve monsters by unlocking next evolution level. Current Monster levels: Slime 1 Level 1

Instances	Able to create parallel realities within the dungeon, allowing for more adventurers to enter the dungeon at the same time
Environments	Able to create new obstacles in the form of environmental hazards.
Locked	Locked

"So, can I get all of them?" Doc asked excitedly.

"Eventually Doc, but not now. Even if you gained power from those men, you still are young and limited in the power you can harness. We can pick maybe two from this list for now, and that's already putting us in the lead of dungeon records for growth speed. After settling with your new abilities, it'll be farming for a long time for us. Adventurers will come in, we fight them, they either die or conquer, and then the whole process will repeat for a long time."

"Okay, I want monster upgrade and instances," Doc said proudly.

Claire clapped her hands, "I'm so proud I didn't have to correct you this time. Yes, those are the best choices for us. Monster upgrade doesn't cost much, and all we have to do is wait for the slimes to evolve on their own. Instance is the big one for us; it'll allow more adventuring and thus more fun!"

"Great, so how do I pay for these things?" Doc deadpanned, "I'm pretty sure I can't pay with gold and silver."

"Nope, you pay with mana capacity."

Doc stared at Claire for a moment. "WHAT!"

Claire winced and rubbed her ears, "What did you expect? Upgrades are improvements to your main body, which means you have to grow in size in order to obtain them. When you add abilities to your repertoire, you take the mana you've earned and actually condense it into new layers for your crystal. Your capacity won't shrink to the point that it affects your current dungeon, but you won't be able to grow it much until more people perish within the dungeon."

Doc sulked.

"Oh! Come off it you silly crystal. Sacrifices need to be made in order to grow. Even the humans have to sacrifice the precious little time they have to live in order to become stronger. In that regard, you aren't that bad off because you can recover your capacity; humans never regain time spent."

Doc still sulked.

"You get to watch new slimes being created," added Claire.

Doc perked up, "You mean without my help?"

Claire nodded, smug, "The upgrade also has a unique effect on each race you acquire it for. For slimes, it has the added bonus of allowing them to split into two slimes when they live long enough. Since we can't afford to actively make them evolve, having evolved slimes split on us is a big help. Do you feel better now?"

"Since I don't have to spend hours making slimes, the answer is yes."

"Don't get your hopes up too high, slimes can only be in one instance at a time. That means you need to make enough slimes for every adventurer group that comes in. Also, the instance upgrade lasts until you reach a certain size sustainable for many groups of adventurers at once."

Doc sighed, and began working on his upgrades and the vast amount of slimes he needed.

Chapter 11

The discovery of Princess Diana, safe outside the dungeon raised a clamor. The letter that was found on her started an uproar that shook the city. Due to her involvement with most sections in the army, the princess was immensely popular with the men in the various factions. Mary was barely able to keep a lid on tensions at the base camp and was forced to send a request for help alongside the report on the princess.

Naturally, the news spread quickly in the city and caused quite the scandal within the nobility. The letter had been signed by the royal seal, a magical artifact that only worked in the hands of an individual with royal blood. There were ways to overcome the magic, but they were rare and expensive to find. Rumors began circulating that at least one member of the royal family was making a power play for the throne. Of a more minor note, the rumors of the mysterious rescuer 'Doc' became a hot topic among the ladies of both common and noble birth. As nothing was known about him, various tales of his dashing nature became popular in the taverns and social gatherings.

In response to the growing tension, King Duran ordered a full investigation into the letter and assigned his best men to track down the culprits responsible. The princess had been conscious long enough to name her attackers before settling back down to rest. The royal physician assured the king that she was merely resting and would awaken eventually.

At the current moment, King Duran and his family were all present in the throne room as the investigators gave their report. Besides King Duran and his wife Queen Nia, also present were First Prince James, Second Prince Marcus, Third Prince Kenneth, First Princess Hilda, and Third Princess Shiva. King Duran had recalled Prince James and Prince Marcus from the royal institute in response to the allegations. The two princes were learning the various skills necessary to run a kingdom, with the understanding that one of them would marry into a different family. The youngest, Princess Shiva, was a young child of 15 years and more interested in boys than anything else. She was a well-known beauty with a flock of admirers that obeyed her every command.

The last investigator finished his report on the letter's destination, explaining how Sir Koran had seen the letter being delivered to his man Hank at night, but had been ignorant of its contents. As the princess hadn't named him as part of the attack, suspicion was lowered around the adventurer, though the king privately made a note to investigate the man further.

"You are dismissed," he said, waving the man away. The knight bowed and left the room. King Duran turned to his family and sighed.

"If any of you have anything to add to this, I will forgive your actions as long as you admit it in the next few minutes."

Hilda, who had been bawling through the entire ordeal, managed to croak out, "She, she asked me for help getting her to the camp. I handed a letter to a guard to deliver to the ranger captain, but the captain told me he never got it."

The queen hugged her daughter closely, cooing sweet words to calm her down. The king sighed wearily as he leaned his face into his hand. Indeed, when asked, the ranger captain revealed he had never heard of the letter in question. His story was verified when the letter was discovered in the garden buried under some freshly moved dirt. Tracking mages had easily found it, but could not locate the guard who should have delivered the letter.

That meant a skilled mage was involved; one with at least the same level of skill as the royal trackers. King Duran groaned as he considered the game being played. "At least it's obvious this wasn't a power play by our family."

Little Shiva turned curiously toward her father. "Why do you say that with such certainty father?"

The king smiled softly at his youngest daughter, "Well, because Diana is very far from inheriting any political power from the throne. James and Marcus are competing against each other for the throne after I retire, and I know she wasn't an important part of eithers' plans."

The brothers nodded, eyeing each other. They shared the most interesting relationship within the family, actively competing against each other in silent battles of influence, wealth, and competitions of strength. Ironically enough, the two liked each other well enough that when the principal heir was announced, the loser would still be happy. He would also still hold sizable influence in the city.

"Kenneth has never wanted power in the city, preferring his ranger duties." King Duran continued. Ken nodded, his desires well known everywhere and by everyone. He had no interest in any matters beyond his military duties, much to the regret of his mother who desired grandchildren.

"Since Diana has never held an interest of courting men or holding political power, I doubt that you, Shiva or Hilda, have any interest in seeing her gone. I expect that with her popularity in the army, she would be an important ally to both of you." King Duran sighed again. Leaning back he added, "Which makes it a mystery of why anyone would want her gone. If other members of the family were also attacked, that would be seen as an effort to destroy the bloodline, but as it stands, besides our reputation, no one else has suffered. To make things worse for the culprit, the men within our forces are surging with bloodlust after hearing about Diana's plight."

"Father." Prince James spoke up, "Would it not be wise to investigate what happened in the dungeon itself?"

The king turned to regard his son, "How so Prince?"

The prince cleared his throat, "The reports state she was found at the entrance days after she entered it. The men who attacked were never found, but according to her, they died the same day they entered. The newest dungeon report states that it has gained the power to create multiple realities within itself, which corroborates her story. I doubt the existence of the so called 'rescuer,' yet someone or something was responsible for her safety. The midwives have confirmed her chastity intact, yet our sister is severely weakened. There is no doubt the letter was used to have an effect on her."

"If the dungeon can hold copies of itself, it is unlikely we would ever find the original tunnel she entered." Prince Marcus spoke up, "That being said, I find myself at the rare opportunity to agree with my fellow prince. The dungeon holds some clues, even if we have to dig it up from the bowels of the earth to find it."

King Duran considered for a moment, "Send trusted men as part of the adventurers' group that will be raiding the dungeon. Have them check for anything unusual while they are down there. Also, keep an eye on Sir Koran. He may seem innocent, but those were his friends who attacked Diana. If anything, a man's company reflects the man himself. I am going to check on my daughter."

Dismissed, the siblings bowed and left the room, Hilda being led by Ken and Shiva. Queen Nia walked over to her husband and took his arm. He smiled up at her, "My dear, the gods know how you are a light upon my life."

She twinkled at him, pulling him up. An accident many years ago had robbed the queen of her voice, but thanks to magical help she was able to speak again with a somewhat normal voice. The king missed her previous sweet voice, but was very happy he could still hear her speak. Even now, though, he could tell how she felt by the color of her eyes; which were currently a deep blue.

"I know my dear; I'm worried for her too." With that, the two left the throne room and headed to the royal infirmary. As it was, the princess was currently the only patient within its walls.

The couple took her hand and bowed their heads, praying to the gods of light for healing and guidance. One of the healers came over to them and bowed to them. "Greetings your royal majesties, I am the healer in charge of the princess." As they were noticeably nervous, the healer quickly continued, "As you can see, she is sleeping soundly and in the process of healing. We have treated her as best we could and limited magical healing to a minimum in order to allow her to recover naturally."

"Naturally, but isn't that terribly slow? Why can you not heal my daughter now?" The King asked frantically."

The healer shook his head, "We dare not heal her body too fast, as her mind is what we worry most about. The letter she was found with most certainly caused her a great deal of grief, so it is important for both her mind and body to heal together so she does not suffer further injury."

"We understand," The King said gravely, taking his sobbing wife into his embrace, "How severe were her injuries?"

The healer turned to the princess and began pointing out the various bandages and wraps, "There were injuries consistent with running and falling from a height, resulting in multiple bruises and a broken arm. From what my assistant has found, the assailants were unable to lay their hands on her directly and we have verified through magic that she remains pure. When she revived, she was barely coherent enough to name her attackers and their claims so her mind seems to be working. Our biggest concern remains that she may have come in to contact with a rare poison or her mind retreats indefinitely into her body. Thankfully from what I have found, she has not been poisoned so her body should recover in time. Her mind on the other hand, that is something we will have to wait and see."

As the Queen sobbed and hugged her child, her body began to glow red as her battle aura came into being. Knowing his wife's temperament when angered, the King quickly hugged her. "Have no fear my love, those responsible will be punished, I assure you." He thanked the healer and promptly led his wife out of the room.

"King husband," The queen growled in anger, "I will personally burn all who dared to lay their hands on my daughter."

He nodded as he walked her swiftly to the training hall where she could take her anger out on the magical dummies. After all, his wife was one of the strongest mages in the kingdom and rarely ever lost her temper. When she did, however, it assuredly spelt disaster for the castle and his coffers.

As the two walked away, a dark-hooded figure stepped out of the shadows and observed them. As the two disappeared around the corner, the figure spoke into a softly glowing stone. "The King remains ignorant of the plan. Shall I execute the princess as a precaution?"

The figure paused for a moment, listening to the response and bowed its head, "As you wish, she shall remain as she is. I will take me leave." It pocketed the stone and led out a quiet growl while eyeing the door to the infirmary where the princess rested. "Curse you child for throwing my plans off. Curse to those fools who failed to carry out their instructions properly, and curse to this mysterious 'Doc'," it growled one more time, "You will regret interfering in this affair, this I assure you."

The figure moved back into the shadow and then it was gone.

Chapter 12

In the coming days, Doc found himself in a predicament. Thanks to his new abilities, he was swarmed with adventurers trying to make a living off of him. He was forced to constantly pop out new slimes at night and he even had to make some during the day. Since the number of parallel realities he could have was unlimited, the tired dungeon lord was forced to use most of his energy creating in order to prevent the more seasoned adventurers from getting too close to his room.

While the majority of adventurers were E through C rank, the B-ranked adventurers from before joined a weaker team and led them to the boss room. It was rare, but occasionally his overslime would be defeated and the herbs would be gathered.

After a week of exploring, various changes took place in the base camp.

The base camp finally finished setting up stores and stalls, creating a miniature town next to the forest. The tavern soon became the most popular spot for adventurers, while the Adventurer Guild outpost was soon assigning various quests to be accomplished.

Due to the nature of Doc's dungeon, the magic enchanting business was doing quite well, attracting various artisans and blacksmiths to the area. The most common weapons were made of copper mined from the dungeon itself. The realities/instances did not start until after the first room, which prevented a surplus of copper and forced the adventurers to assign times for when individuals could mine.

The dungeon underwent a few changes as well, mostly in the variety of slimes. With the first evolution perk unlocked, some of Doc's slimes had undergone evolution and propagated. The most common evolution was the herb slime: a slime created after ingesting a certain amount of herb plants form the heart room. They gained a green color and abilities to poison or paralyze their prey by shooting small bits of themselves. Their loot expanded to include a slime extract that was used in remedies for poison and paralyses.

The second slime type that arose came from the pitfall traps where a few unlucky/dumb/'accidentally pushed' fell in and were devoured. This led to the evolution of hungry slimes: pale purple slimes with a hint of grey that actively hunted humans. According to Claire, they were the first step toward gelatinous slimes and had a more intelligent instinct to ambush prey. They also had an increased defense toward physical weapons, though magic still killed them quickly.

The last slime was the rarest form. It arose from slimes that actively ate a variety of living things. Humans and the occasional elf were not the only things to enter Doc's dungeon; sometimes, rats, bugs, bats, birds, and other animals entered as well.

The animals somehow bypassed the instances, but were usually promptly eaten. This led to the evolution of a lesser mimic slime that arose from the variety: blue slimes that could change their form to whatever they had previously eaten. They were weak because they were small and could only copy the form and abilities of anything smaller than themselves. The only exception was a slightly larger blue slime that slept in Claire's house. She had somehow gotten it to change into a bed, and slept on it.

The two new slimes types dropped parts of whatever they had previously eaten, including armor from the hungry slimes and animal parts from the mimics. This increased the value of his dungeon, and thus improved the town's commerce as well. Besides that, there was a curious amount of female adventurers who seemed hell bent on finding something. They always left disappointed; however, that never stopped them from coming back.

Doc sighed as he felt the last adventurer group leave his dungeon. He slid into the overslime and relaxed until the slime was a puddle on the floor. Claire flew out of her home and flew over him in circles. "Oh my, Doc, you're melted! Is having a body really such a relaxing thing for you?"

Doc sighed contently, "Being me means I can stay awake and concentrate, but being a slime lets me lose focus and rest. It's a really nice thing, kind of like the baths you take."

Claire turned red, "Do you watch me take a bath? You...!"

"What are you talking about?" Doc asked, "You know I don't watch your home unless invited. You're the one always talking about how nice a bath is. Anyway, why is watching you take a bath bad?"

Claire coughed awkwardly, "Well, it's the same feeling as if a person handled your real body."

Doc imagined for a moment, "Okay then, I'll be sure to never watch you bathe. Anyway, how do you think I'm doing as a dungeon?"

Claire landed on the edge of her pedestal and stretched her arms and legs. "Well, you have a good setup going here. The adventurers are happy, the slimes are evolving, and you are gaining a little magic power from every adventurer." She paused, nodding to herself, "I was surprised when you figured out how to passively absorb mana from adventurers on your own."

Doc smiled, "Since I'm kind of averse to killing, it seemed like an obvious thing to try out."

"They still die though," said Claire.

"Yeah, but I don't cause it. I just don't stop it," Doc said.

They shared a slight chuckle. Besides the one incident, Doc hadn't felt the same rush of emotion he had when he had seen the princess in trouble. A few of the women adventurer groups had had accidents and "accidents," but he viewed them with the same indifference he had the men. Only one C-ranked adventurer had fallen in his dungeon, and that had not provided a significant boost to his mana capacity; none had the smatterings of E and D-ranked adventurers. The cost had decreased his magical reservoir to slightly less than his original amount before the death of the B-ranked jerks, and he had just now only approached his original level.

Claire, of course, kept up reminding him that his growth was substantial for a new dungeon. He still sulked a little bit, though on the inside, but was pleased with the new size of his core. Now he had doubled his previous body in size and was larger than Claire, which was a private victory.

"It is kind of boring though," he commented from the ground, "They mostly come in for the copper now, and few actually try to get to my herbs. Killing the herb slimes seem to be enough for them these days."

Claire nodded, "I agree, we need to come up with a better reward to encourage the greedier adventurers to come deeper."

They thought together for a while, tossing ideas back and forth. Claire dismissed his idea for gold mines, citing that the greed would be too great and his walls would be mined to death. Doc disagreed with her idea of creating pet slimes to be claimed arguing successfully that he didn't want to give slimes away; besides, he had no idea how to in the first place. After a couple more ridiculous ideas, the two sighed and took a small break.

"Why don't we make better herbs?" He asked from his floor.

"Because we can't grow anything silly. Remember, I got those herbs from the forest myself. Now I can't leave because of the danger from those people outside."

Doc pondered for a moment, "Why don't I make a small path for you to the forest?"

Claire's mouth fell open, "Err… I… um… yeah, that could work."

"Great!" Doc smiled, "I'll get right on it." As he turned his attention away, Claire's smile slipped from her face as she began to sniff and hugged her legs to her chest. Startled by the sound, Doc looked back just in time to watch the tears forming in her eyes.

"Claire, why are you sad?" he asked her with concern.

Even though she was right next to him, she gave no sign she had heard him. Instead, she flew to the corner and began muttering to herself. Doc listened closely to her as she muttered, "Failure, I'm such a failure. Such a simple solution and I couldn't think of it. How can I call myself useful if I don't think of these things?"

Concerned over her sudden depression, Doc quickly created a new slime and had it drop onto her from above. Startled by the sudden entrance, Claire struggled to escape her new slimy prison as she stared around wildly.

"Enough of that Claire!" He commanded. "You are my only friend and the only reason I've gotten this far. I don't know why you're strange, but I'll punish you if you ever say you aren't good enough again."

Doc then had the slime unceremoniously spit the tiny pixie out onto the floor. Still in a slight shock from the experience of being eaten by a slime, Claire paused long enough to ask, "What kind of punishment?"

Doc paused, obviously not expecting to give an actual answer. "Um... I'll watch you bathe in your bath suit." Claire had told him about the outfit she wore during her baths once, but he had never seen it himself.

The little purple fairy turned into a bright red fireball as she raced around the room, shouting things that offended Doc's non-existent ears. Out of reflex, he made tentacles to cover where he instinctively thought his ears were. Of course, as a slime, sound traveled through his body like he was made of water, so the action was pointless.

"Okay, okay, okay!" He shouted, "I won't do that!" He relaxed as Claire calmed down and returned to her natural purple color. "Seriously, was it that bad of a punishment?"

"Yes, you dummy! I don't want my naked body to be seen!"

"Naked?"

"Without my clothes."

"What are clothes?"

She pointed at her dress.

"Oh, I thought that was another slime sticking to you," Doc replied.

"..."

Doc had a sudden thought, "So, am I naked too? Do I have to cover my crystal body?"

Claire began to giggle uncontrollably, amazed by the whole situation. "No, you silly! You don't need to. You don't have parts to cover up."

"Why would anyone want to cover themselves?" Doc asked confused. "Are parts valuable treasure or something?"

Claire paused. "I have no idea. Mommy never got to explaining it to me before I left. I just know she told me to never let anyone look at me in the bath besides other girls and a special person. Though she did say some things that sounded like treasure; balls of gold and orbs of man's desire."

With a sad sigh, Doc said "I guess I'm not special enough for you."

Claire blushed furiously, but became thoughtful. "I guess that's true; you are the most special person to me. Okay, you can watch when I wear my bath suit." She lowered her voice, "But please let me know, okay?"

"Okay." Doc was happy again. He then became serious, "Now, tell me, why you got so depressed earlier? I've never seen you like that, and it seems kind of out of character."

Claire frowned and crossed her arms as she thought to herself. She shook her head, "I'm not too sure myself. To be perfectly honest, I don't have a clear memory, even though it just happened. This is very strange; especially since this isn't the first time you've suggested a better way of doing things."

They both 'hmmed' for a while, then shrugged and filed the incident away for later. Since both of them were not that experienced, whenever they could not figure certain things out, they would put them away for later dates.

"Ready for your forest tunnel?" Doc asked.

"Yup!" said Claire eagerly.

Using his mana, Doc expanded his influence down from the dungeon to create a pixie sized tunnel that came up in the forest a safe distance from any human activity. Thanks to all the practiced he had done he was able to finish quickly and even had time to add a little stone door in her house that opened into it. Claire happily thanked him and promptly flew into her home and down the new tunnel.

He followed her down the tunnel, but the farther he got the more sluggish his mind felt. "Sorry Claire, I can't go much farther."

"It's okay," she thought back, "I'll be careful. Just watch from there and let me know if you sense anyone coming."

She flew out the exit and began searching the forest in the rapidly approaching twilight. Doc felt increasing frustration as she cooed and awed at every little thing she saw while collecting a variety of plant sprouts.

"Hurry up! I don't like being away for too long."

She stuck her tongue at him, "It's important that I take my time in this decision. I have to pool all my options together and then narrow them down to what I think is best. Oh, what a pretty flower!"

Doc mentally slapped his crystal at her actions. He groaned, and then paused as he felt something.

"Claire, something is coming this way." He frowned as he felt the vibrations in the earth, "It feels like horses, but smaller."

Instantly, she flew back over to him, holding as many plants as she could carry. "Close the tunnel, close the tunnel!" She cried out as she entered the tunnel.

While confused, Doc obeyed and closed the tunnel with stone. Once it was done, Claire breathed out in relief as her legs failed and she sat on the ground.

"What was coming?" He asked her.

Claire shuddered visibly, "Wolves; those were wolves in the woods. Wolves are a type of predator that hunt in packs. All the new activity from the adventurers must have attracted them to the area."

"What do they look like?" He asked curiously.

"You don't have anything to imagine them with," she explained, "It's better to wait till they get closer to you and then you can see them for yourself."

"Can the slimes eat them?"

"I doubt the mimics will be able to, but your overslime should have no problem. Like all monsters and animals, the wolves will be naturally drawn to the magical nature of your dungeon for safety. You'll have to decide what to do with them then; whether to keep them or eat them. I had a relative who was eaten by a wild wolf, so I'll be hiding when they come in initially."

Doc nodded, "Okay, I'll worry about that later. Did you get anything useful?"

Holding out a thumbs up, Claire smiled in satisfaction as she examined the plants, "I did indeed. The herbs you currently have are uncommon, but are still ranked "E" herbs. I managed to get a few D-ranked poisons, and this." She held out a tiny sprout that glowed softly, "This is a C-ranked plant known as Moonglow. It's only found during the full moon, so we got really lucky. The herbalists would love to get even a small bit of it for potions and the like."

"Great! Let's plant it in the room on the ceiling so it can light the room some. A lot of the adventurers are complaining about the dim purple light."

Claire rolled her eyes, "Of course they are, silly, purple light is bothersome to most eyes after all. Just use the torches from the dead adventurers and put them in your walls."

"Oh, that makes sense."

They headed back together as the sun finally winked out of the sky. A long howl filled the woods, and the night came to life.

Chapter 13

The following day, a group of adventurers approached the dungeon entrance. They were a small group of five members, led by a tall red haired lady warrior named Fiora. She was a C rank adventurer who was well experienced with battle and had confidently led her friends through many trials. She wore a heavy iron armor that never hindered her grace and speed and carried a sword and shield on her back.

Following Fiora were her comrades in arms who had lived with her through thick and thin. First, there were the twin warriors Nick and Natalie. The brother went by the nickname Nic and his sister preferred to be called Nat. The twins focused on strength to balance with Fiora's defense, and could wield a small amount of fire and water buffing magic respectively. The brown-haired, blue-eyed, 20 year-old humans were still in their prime and hungered for adventures.

Joining them from the Mage University was the human mage Jonas, a smaller man who preferred reading to traveling. He used to join the group reluctantly, usually dragged along by his best friend Nic, but after living through one life threatening situation after another, the man had become used to them and now looked forward to any magical discoveries they made.

The last member of their group was an elf named Gran. An archer in practice, but also served as the healer of the group, specializing in potions and battle remedies. Gran was a young elf, a little over 100, and had joined Fiora after one of her guild assignments had resulted in his life being saved. His life debt to her had long since been paid off, but he had found that he quite enjoyed traveling and adventuring so he had chosen to stay with them.

Today, the group had decided they were going to fight to the bottom of the dungeon and defeat the dungeon boss as a challenge. It was well known that while interesting, the herbs earned by defeating the dungeon boss were often not worth the risk in getting there.

As they reached the entrance, Fiora turned and surveyed the group. "Do we have everything ready for this?" She asked.

Gran nodded, "I have potions for slime burn and minor injuries. My arrows have been enchanted as well."

Jonas nodded, "I also took the time to enchant the twins' weapons. My magic is ready as well for the battle ahead."

The twins drew their swords and nodded. They were eager to begin exploring the dungeon. Fiora cracked a grin at their eagerness. "Remember, this is a slime dungeon; it is unique and should not be underestimated. Reports have confirmed its growth and new enemies within, so stay sharp."

With that, she turned and entered the dungeon. The others quickly followed her as Gran cast light-balls to light their way.

It was well known that the initial tunnel was clear of enemies, but they did not drop their guard as they slowly walked down the path. The walls glowed with a soft purple light as water dripped from spots on the ceiling to the floor. Fiora eyed the various puddles in their path. "Gran, any chance you can verify those aren't slimes?"

He shook his head, "Besides wasting magic to disturb the water or risking equipment to poke them, I cannot. The magic tool used to inspect dungeons was returned to the main guild branch after it was used by the scouting team. It's a unique, old magic tool that hasn't been replicated yet, and the death of the team has made the administration nervous enough to devout more research into it."

Nat sneered, "I heard that their deaths were well-deserved after their attack on the princess. Sir

Koran has always had a questionable reputation, and now his men have shown their true nature. I can't wait till a reward is assigned for his arrest."

Nic patted his sister as the group moved forward slowly, "There is no proof yet of his involvement, only that he knew of the letter's existence and that his men read it."

"Of course he knew what was in the letter! Those friends of his would never act without his approval!"

"Perhaps, Sister, but we cannot prove anything, and his father is putting pressure to leave Koran out of the investigation."

Fiora listened but did not comment. Privately, she agreed with the idea that Sir Koran was involved, but she knew that he was too cunning to have left any proof of his involvement. It would have been a favor to the world if he had disappeared along with his men.

Gran used his bow to shoot each puddle, but none of them held a slime and the group exited the tunnel safely. The first room glittered with veins of copper that ran through the wall. None of them had any interest in the metal, so they quickly left the room and entered the "real" dungeon. As they exited the room, they felt the magic energy shift around them.

"Okay, prepare for battle!" Fiora announced as she drew the sword and shield. Surprisingly, torches were now embedded in the walls at intervals and cast a fiery light down the dungeon tunnel. It gave a better view of the surroundings, much better than the normal purple glow that had been expected.

"My lady, there are slimes approaching," Gran announced, drawing back his bow. Three slimes slid down the walls toward them, each a purple color. Gran released his arrows and hit the cores of each of them with pinpoint accuracy.

Jonas inspected them, "These are the common slime of the dungeon," he announced. "Very weak to anything magic."

Nic raised an eyebrow, "I've never heard of the slimes moving toward us like this. They should be hidden for ambushes instead."

Jonas nodded as he got back up, "That is true, but if their previous places have new occupants then the slimes would be forced to move."

Nat gasped, "Are you saying that the slimes were forced to move because of stronger monsters?"

Jonas added, "Most likely, but there are other possible reasons for the move. In any case, we should be wary for new dangers."

The group collected the slime cores and proceeded down the hallway. They moved together in formation to keep an eye out for ambushes: Nic kept his eyes on the ceiling, Nat kept her eyes on the floor, Jonas extended his magic senses around them, and Gran used his ears to listen.

While the others concentrated on the different areas around the group, Fiora kept her eyes staring ahead down the tunnel. She stepped her foot down just as Jonas grabbed her arm. Her foot paused on the surface as she turned to regard the mage.

"There is a pitfall in front of you," he explained, "Be careful where you step."

Nodding, Fiora moved her foot back as she slammed the butt of her sword into the ground. The fragile stone crumbled away to reveal a round hole that descended a few feet down into darkness. Jonas sent a light-orb down and illuminated the gray-purple slimes lying in wait.

"Those are the new species of slime." Gran announced, "Grey slimes are highly resistant to anything physical, even magic infused weapons."

"Will they chase us?" Nat asked, eyeing the still slimes.

Gran shook his head, "They will only chase if disturbed. As long as none of us fall in, they will remain there. I advise we save our mage for moving threats."

Nodding in agreement, the group moved around the pitfall and continued their way. They encountered two more slime pitfalls, each on opposite sides of the tunnel. Each time, Jonas warned Fiora, who then broke the covering and revealed more grey slimes.

They reached the second room and paused outside. "The report suggests the room has slimes on the ceiling," Fiora reiterated, "So it's important we don't fall prey to ambush." She poked her sword into the room experimentally and swung it around. Nothing happened and she pulled her arm back into the tunnel.

Sighing, Fiora put her shield over her head and ran into the room as fast as she could. She ran straight through, keeping her shield over her head as she heard the tell-tale noises of slimes disconnecting from the ceiling. As she ran, one slime dropped right in front of her. Not pausing, she jumped over the slime and kept on moving. As she neared the other side, she felt a slime land on top of her shield. The shield was enchanted to prevent it from being eaten or dissolved, but the sudden increase in weight fumbled her hand and caused her to become momentarily distracted. She tripped over another slime and slammed into the ground near the next tunnel.

Her reflexes kicked in, honed through many battles, and she rolled away to her left, dodging a slime that had fallen on her downed position. She leaped up and drew her sword as she backed toward the hall. Her friends called out to her from the other side, but were too distracted by their own slimes to help.

She eyed the monsters before her. These slimes were blue, signaling another new species; one that she unfortunately had no experience with. Before her eyes, the slimes shook and changed into blue insects. The bug slimes were strange; possessing all the parts of a bug, but at the same time did not resemble any one type. She could see locusts, beetles, and ants intermingled together as they marched toward her.

"They are lesser mimic slimes!" She heard Jonas call to her, "They can move the same way as their form, but are still slimes."

"Good to know," she thought wryly to herself, taking a ready position.

The bugs swarmed her, jumping and snapping at her. Taking a deep breath, Fiora swung her blade as a locust slime leapt at her, cutting through its core. She twirled around and cut the heads off two ant mimics at her feet. Their bodies regrew heads and resumed their attack on her.

Cursing, she threw a fire potion at them and rolled to her shield. The potion exploded in fiery death as the mimic slimes dissolved under its oppressive heat. She sliced the beetle slime on her shield and picked it up just in time to bash another locust mimic into the floor. Using the flat shield as a base, she spun it and stood on one arm as her sword cut two beetle slimes down their middle. She flipped back and moved her sword arm behind her.

Focusing her mana, she infused the sword with fire and lashed out in an arc in front of her. The sword released a wave of fire that melted the slimes in front of her. A pain on her leg alerted her to an ant slime that had made its way through to her body. Wincing, she sliced its core and backed up to the wall.

As the remaining few slimes approached her, arrows hit each of them and killed them as she watched. Sighing in relief, she slid to the floor and let her breath escape her.

Gran hurried over to her, taking out a potion as he knelt down. "The good news is that it didn't break the skin." he reported. He inspected the bite closely - it was between her armor plates - "The mimics can't make themselves sharp, which is a small blessing," he added while dabbing the slime burn potion on her, and she sighed as the burning sensation faded away.

Nat glared at Fiora as Nic and Gran helped her up, "Fearless leader, I really wish you wouldn't act according to your title. I was really scared for a moment."

Fiora chuckled, "In truth, so was I. I even had to use one of my fire potions to escape." She frowned at her belt. Fire potions were useful for dealing with crowds, but the ingredients for it were found in the mountainous regions, far from the plains, and had to be shipped at cost to the city. They didn't come cheap enough to buy in loads, but every experienced adventurer carried at least two at all times.

Jonas inspected the dissolving slime as it faded away, "None of the reports ever mentioned mimic slimes. Herb and Grey slimes were thought to be the only new varieties, but I guess that isn't true, is it? In any case, the guild will pay for this new information." He picked up a slime core and a beetle shell. "The shell is slightly bigger after being eaten by the slime it seems. If memory serves, these shells can be used in certain paints if enough are gathered," he added.

Nic snorted in amusement, "How would a beetle shell be used for paint?"

Jonas held the shell up to a torch and moved it. The shell twinkled red in the torchlight. "As you can see, this is from a red beetle. When crushed, the shell produces a red pigment that can be used to create red paints. The beetle isn't from the area though; it originates from the more lush forests to the south. I'd say one of our merchants misplaced a shipment of them and they ended up in the dungeon to be eaten. The other parts have their own uses as well."

Nat frowned at the scattered cores and loot, "Gross! Insects are disgusting and I don't want to have anything to do with them," she said, and folded her arms while staring at her brother down on the floor holding his hands up in a pleading gesture.

"No one is making you collect the parts. Tell you what, you watch our fearless leader and we men will collect them okay?"

The girls had a fun time pointing out every locust leg or ant mandible the guys missed. The group decided it was more prudent to go back and report their findings to the guild as soon as possible to prevent less experienced adventurers from falling to the new species.

Later that day, the guild announced that the dungeon difficulty had been raised from E to D, and

E-ranked adventurers were not permitted to enter unless escorted by someone of a higher rank.

Chapter 14

"Are you ready Claire?"

"I think so Doc," she said timidly.

"Are you sure? I don't want to force you to do this."

She gave him a kind, but determined look, "Doc, you have to do this. Make yourself into a man!"

Doc gave her a droll look, "I'm not human you know."

"Idiot! You're male so act like it! Come on, I'm a big girl!" Emotions rising, Doc nodded, "Fine, you asked for it. Today, I become a man and you a woman!" Claire swooned, "Oh my, what a declaration!"

"Take it Claire, take it all!"

"Oh, oh, OH DOC!"

"CLAIRE!"

***

The two relaxed in Claire's bedroom, Doc inhabiting her slime bed. Claire smiled and rolled over on him, rubbing his 'back' affectionately. "Doc, that was the best I've ever seen."

"You think so? I've never tried it before, so I wasn't sure I'd be any good."

She scoffed and giggled, "No problem there, you were great!"

"Thank you so much for helping me install that shelf in my wall."

Doc flexed his slime tentacle in an effort to copy a human habit he had observed. "I wasn't positive I could control this body properly and was really scared I'd break it. I'm happy it worked out."

"Me too." The two smiled happily at the new wood shelf in the bedroom. Claire had used her magic to form the shelf from scraps of torch, but had needed Doc's strength to put it in the wall. Sure he could have adsorbed the wall and placed it himself as a dungeon, but Claire didn't want his influence in her home. Not that she minded his presence, but she wanted everything to be done without magic in her house.

Doc didn't quite understand, but he did relish the challenge of delicate work. The shelf was rather fragile, being composed of various wood fragments stuck together, and his tentacle had not been intended for usage beyond whipping and sticking.

"I'm proud to say that you've mastered an important part of having a dungeon boss," Claire declared, "Fine control over your body. Being able to control the lesser abilities of your body will assist you in future battles."

"I don't see it," Doc declared flatly, "Shouldn't combat be about overpowering your enemy?"

Claire waved her hand as she rolled onto her back, "For basic combat, yes, but the stronger the enemies you face, the more you'll find agility, reflexes, and experience; that will serve you better than raw strength like, for instance, being able to control more tentacles."

Doc perked up in interest, "So the better I control my body, the more things I can do with it?"

"Yup, that is it exactly right!" Claire giggled and rolled around on his "back." "Slimes don't really need lots of control because they lack a lot of the equipment other monsters and sentient beings have, like fingers, for instance." She wiggled her fingers and rubbed the bed.

"Fingers... I want them." Doc declared. He moved away and entered the overslime. Wiggling out a tentacle, he focused on it with the utmost concentration. A tiny slime tentacle popped out the end, and then another one appeared, and then another. He ended up with five tiny slime tentacles at the end of his regular tentacle.

"Now, let's see what I can do." He tried to move the tentacles, but only managed to wiggle them in waves. Frustrated, Doc tired again, and the tentacles stuck together. He growled mentally as he waved it around in frustration, but only managed to sink the tentacle back into his arm.

Claire watched amusedly from her perch as he struggled for a while to make fingers. "Are you having fun yet?" She asked him after he calmed down.

"I can't make them work like yours," he complained, eyeing the stubborn tentacle, "I can't make them separate and move by themselves."

Claire shrugged and floated down to his head, "You can't expect to know what you don't know," she said sagely, "My mommy used to tell me that when I asked her complicated things, like baby making. You've never had fingers, so how should you know how they work?"

"Oh," Doc said sadly, "That's disappointing."

Claire patted him, "Don't worry Doc, I'm sure you'll figure out fingers someday. After all, there are many rumors in the world about highly dangerous monsters, which include tales of human-shaped slimes.

Doc stared at her, "What's significant about that? If I wanted to, I could have a slime take the form of a human. It may take a while and prevent it from moving around, but it would be doable."

Claire started, "Well, that is true I guess, but why do something wasteful like that? Anyway, I guess I need to tell you the tales in full for you to understand." She flew up to her perch and sat down, clearing her throat."

"As you know already, adventurers of all races rate themselves on their system of strength from rank E to rank A. There are three ranks above A and they are not commonly used for adventurers; these are rank S, rank SS, and rank SSS. There are a limited number of S-ranked adventurers, but I have never heard of any above that level. Those ranks exist because this classification system is also used for monsters, slimes included. The slimes that take human form are said to be SS rank monsters, some of the most dangerous in existence. They are immune to physical damage, have the ability to split, and are very intelligent, which is nearly on par with normal adventurers. Slimes, even the low ranking ones, are always dangerous because of their abilities, but lack a clear advantage because of their lack of brain or ability to plan. You can see what I am getting at here."

Doc flip-flopped up and down in excitement, "That is amazing! That means that slimes are a worthy existence in this world, up there with the top monsters right?"

"Nope."

"Eh?"

Claire shrugged her hands, "As I said, it's a legend. In other words, no one knows the truth and the rumors can't be verified. If there are slimes like that out there, they do a wonderful job hiding themselves from the rest of the world. If they do exist, then they are very far down the evolutionary path we are currently on. My advice is to wait and see."

"That's disappointing to hear," Doc lamented, "Is there anything else you can tell about them that's vaguely known?"

Claire nodded, "If they are immune to physical damage, then that means they lack a core. Gelatinous slimes share that ability, so perhaps it exists further down that particular path. Also, their form ability would be related to the lesser mimic slimes, presenting another possible path."

"Don't slimes need cores to exist?"

Claire waved her hand, "Most slimes have some sort of core, but some do not need it. As I just said, the gelatinous slime I told you about doesn't have a core, which is why it's immune to anything physical.

The core is the center of the slime and thus is responsible for controlling the mucous slime around it. Without it, the slime dissolves and no longer lives. Gelatinous slimes and their relatives actually dissolve their core within their own bodies, pulling apart every inch of their body to remove that weakness. They are the only monster known to have that ability."

"Other monsters have cores in them?" Doc was very surprised.

Claire snorted, "I'm sorry, that's a half truth. Monsters have a part inside them that is involved in the use and storage of mana. When killed, it can be removed and used by certain people. Those are normally referred to as magic hearts or 'cores'."

"So monsters have cores/magic hearts," Doc mused, "and the sentient races don't have cores because they conduct magic naturally?"

"Something like that," Claire agreed, "Mommy wasn't quite sure how to explain it either. Something to do with a "fun-da-me-nal" thingy that makes races, races, and monsters, monsters."

"You keep saying you mother taught you things, but didn't the dungeon teach you anything?" He asked curiously.

"Nope, the dungeon tried to eat me," Claire declared nonchalantly.

"WHAT!" Doc shouted in shock.

"Well, what did you expect?" Claire asked confusedly, "Dungeons aren't born smart; they are born of instinct. The only thing they don't try to eat is their bonded Dungeon Pixie, and that's because of the magic linking the two together. Everything else within a dungeon is fair game, except in the Dungeon Pixie's home."

"Oh, is that why you don't want me in your part of the dungeon?" Doc realized.

Claire nodded, "Yup, that's the reason, indeed. I know you wouldn't eat my children, but I have to teach them eventually."

Doc digested this information, "So, your dungeon really tried to eat you."

"I was smaller and I wanted to explore the dungeon. A scary zombie tried to bite me, but mommy saved me by distracting it." Claire frowned, "But, I don't…remember it very well for some reason."

"You know Claire; everything you've said about dungeons so far has led me to believe they were all like me," Doc said slowly, "But now you're saying other dungeons are dangerous places because they can devour everything."

Claire's frown grew as she began to rub her head, "My head hurts."

"Why did you lie to me Claire, or did you not realize what you were doing?" Doc sensed her growing confusion and stress.

Claire grimaced, stood up, and began pacing. "Mommy saved me, but I wasn't in danger. Dungeons aren't dangerous, dungeons are friends. Scary zombies are scary... really scary." She began to vibrate, her tiny form shaking on the pedestal.

Doc began to grow more concerned, "Claire, what's wrong?"

She began muttering to herself, and Doc recognized the feeling. It was similar to an earlier one when he had a better idea than her. Whatever the matter, it was inside Claire's head and he was helpless to assist her.

As she paced, her foot slipped off the edge and, with a cry, fell off the pedestal. Doc waited a second, than shot forward when her wings didn't work to catch her. His tentacle caught her before she hit the floor, and he brought her to him. The little pixie was crying and gasping as she twitched in his tentacle. Not knowing what else to do, he brought her to his body and hugged her.

"It's okay Claire, I'm here. Don't fear anything anymore, alright?" Overcome with a feeling, he began singing to her. The noise began in his heart, and flowed out through the bond to her. It flowed into his body as every slime began to vibrate in the dungeon. The adventurers watched in wonder as all the slimes paused and began vibrating in song. Music flowed through the dungeon:

Sleep little child, never cry again
Lonely nights are gone, happiness awaits.
Moonlight calls down, sinking peacefully
Stars call your name, and the sun sleeps with you too.
Express what is known,
Relive what's yet to come
Believe in what is shown
For life is not only for some
Life is the wind, the ocean, and storm

As solid as the earth and moon.
Black as night, pure as white,
The opposite of death's embrace

Claire calmed down as Doc finished singing, eyeing him through tears as she hugged him with all her might. "I'm sorry Doc, I'm really, really sorry." She sobbed.

Doc patted her gently with his tentacle (it did come in handy after all). "It's okay little Claire, but tell me why you are so sorry."

She sniffed, "Mommy put a memory spell on me after I was attacked. She was scared the fear would eat me up forever, so she cast the spell to make me forget until I bonded with a dungeon. It wasn't a zombie that attacked me; it was the dungeon boss itself. A tall, dark skeletal knight that oozed miasma and death. I'd lived in the home my whole life, and had never been scared like that before. The spell messed up, but t wasn't apparent until I bonded with you. Since you were already sentient, it started to cover more memories than it was supposed to. Its original intention was to keep me happy and eager to bond with a dungeon. I'm sorry I messed up; I'm really, really sorry." Her lips trembled as she hugged the gelatinous mass.

Doc eyed the little pixie and felt for her. He hugged her childish self to him and said, "I forgive you, alright? It wasn't your fault little one, so no harm. After all, I'm so much bigger than you; it's my responsibility to take care of you."

She giggled amidst her sobs, "Silly, I'm the same size as you!"

He chuckled, "I doubled in size remember? Now I'm bigger than you."

"Stupid." She beat her fist against him, "Stupid Doc's not bigger than me." She eyed him angrily and before his eyes grew an inch, doubling her previous size. She grinned, than resumed her hug.

"Silly dummy Doc, we're always the same, forever and ever."

Chapter 15

Mary scratched her head as she gathered the reports together on her desk. Thanks to the success of farming the dungeon, the previous 'tent city' had finally blossomed into a proper town on the edge of the forest. It was still mostly populated by humans, and many supplies had to be shipped in from Duran, but proper buildings and a wooden palisade had been built. The Adventurer Guild Branch office also experienced a change as the building had been completed and Mary had moved into her new personal office on the second floor. The magic torches flickered overhead, casting a low light in the room as the sun was setting through the window behind her. Sighing, she read the summary reports on the dungeon in front of her.

Account #25

Dungeon confirmed as being of difficulty rank E with magic required.

Boss confirmed as Overslime variant magic attribute.

Account #135

Dungeon complexity increased as of day 75 in the year 2032.

Confirmed the presence of multiple realities within the dungeon

Confirmed new evolutionary slimes within the dungeon

Account #141

Unusual situation occurred within the dungeon.

Multiple adventurers in different realities within the dungeon reported phenomena.

Locals have taken to calling the event the 'Choir of the Slimes."

Slimes reportedly stopped attacking and began emitting musical tones with their bodies.

Slimes did not defend or attack during the event and were easily claimed by all adventurers.

Reasons for the event remain unknown.

Mary rubbed her head as she placed the summaries on top of the official reports. She regretted her previous views about been banished here, as she now was one of the most important people in Duran with her influence in the dungeon town. Privately, she had come to accept the boring assignment and thought the job would allow her more freedom to train and entertain herself, but now the dungeon seemed to have something new to report on every day. Not only had three new species appeared within it, but the last adventurer team to beat the endboss had returned with Moonglow of all things.

"And now the dungeon sings." She chuckled as she stacked the papers together, "Will wonders ever cease?"

A knock at her door broke her train of thought. "Enter," she called out.

Fiora the Fearless entered the office, her long hair tied in braids down her back. The adventurer had once been a part of Mary's group back before she retired, and the two had kept up the friendship even after Mary became an administrator. Mary was well versed with the reasons for Fiora's title, and could smile ruefully as she took in the sight of the woman before her.

"For the gods' sake," she shook her head, "Do you even try to protect yourself?" Fiora had an arm in a sling and numerous small bandages around her body. Fiora smiled ruefully at her and shrugged.

"You should know better than to ask that. Who was it that beat me till I was black and blue in sparring and yelled at me to use my shield?" The two shared a laugh of nostalgia, thinking back to when the fearless leader had been a fearless, obstinate teenager.

Fiora gestured toward her arm, "The overslime had a few new tricks this time. It picked me up with a tentacle and threw me into the wall. Nothing a little grog and healer can't fix."

Mary groaned and clutched her head with both hands. "Not again," she muttered as she began writing on a new sheet of parchment, "Now I have to rewrite the report to include that. You have your report on its new abilities?"

Fiora nodded and took a sheet of paper out of her sling. As she handed the report over, she asked, "Why don't you use your elvish magic to write it? I cringe just imagining doing your job."

Mary gave her a droll stare, "Not all of us get headaches after only a few hours of reading and writing. Besides, you know that there is no 'elvish spell for writing'," Mary air-quoted with her fingers, "Especially since elves prefer to remember through words rather than literature; besides, no reason to show off my mixed blood any more than I have to."

She sighed and waved vaguely at the wall, "It was bad enough they tricked me into coming out here; now some of the other administrators are pressuring the guild master to replace me with someone less... I don't need anyone giving me contempt for 'elf favoring'."

Fiora sighed and leaned back into her chair, "You know the guild master would never exile you, and he would never have you replaced after everyone gave such 'heartfelt' approval for it. Those leeches are merely green with envy at your good fortune and won't be able to get anything but scraps from this. Besides, everyone in town loves you and would never think anything bad of you."

Mary snorted, "The key word you missed in that sentence was 'most.' You know Koran and the group he's part of loathe mixed bloods and sympathizers. The little bastard is still trying to get into my robes, you know."

"Typical hypocrite behavior; willing to set aside for pleasure, but not for love," Fiora waved her hand, "On a more relevant topic, here is the Moonglow we collected from the dungeon boss." She took out the herb and placed it on the desk. The Moonglow was a white flower that closed into a long dipper form in the daylight. It could be used like this, but its beauty only appeared during the full moon. Right now, it would be impossible to differentiate it from a regular droop herb, which was very common in the area.

"I still can't believe Moonglow actually bloomed in the dungeon." Mary couldn't hold back her wonder as she inspected the plant, "When news of this spreads, medicine makers will flock to the area to buy as much as they can."

"I wouldn't hold my breath on that," Fiora spoke up, "The fight was harder this time, and there wasn't that much Moonglow there. We took a single plant, but only the flower itself is needed for potion making. If adventurers run to their death dying against the boss, even if they survived I doubt a single flower would earn them much."

Mary waved her hand, "A single flower can be used to make at least five potions if properly handled. Since you brought back the whole plant, I'm sure someone will be willing to pay well for this little wonder. We'll limit requests to only acquiring the flowers so the dungeon can regrow them. Anyway, what kinds of requests are being posted on The Board?"

The Board was the large wall where anyone could post requests for the guild members after leaving some type of reward at the guild. Adventurers would take the request they wanted, and would turn the notice in with the proof they had for completing the quest. The receptionist would then give the adventurers the reward for the job. Mary had been stuck writing reports for the past few days, and had been unable to check on it herself.

Fiora tapped her chin in thought, "Well, the requests haven't changed too much since you last saw them. Collecting quests are one of the highest still; lots of workers are asking for copper from the mine. A few want herbs from the dungeon boss room, but the reward really isn't enticing enough to attract many of us. Now that I think about it, there are a few new subjugation quests that have appeared."

Mary raised an eyebrow.

"Some wolves have begun to appear from the forest," Fiora explained, "They have been stealing some of the livestock brought in from the city. They have become a large enough nuisance that a reward was offered for their pelts. There's also a rumor going around that a demon was spotted during the full moon, but nothing has been confirmed as of now. Lastly, one of the old fossils from the wizard council offered a reward for an intact slime."

Mary and Fiora looked at each other, and burst out laughing. Mary snorted and giggled as she collected herself, "Oh, I love the wizard council! They come up with the most ridiculous requests and outrageous rewards. What did they offer this time?"

Fiora laughed, "They offered to perform a familiar contract for free with the slime, with the added bonus of being an untested experiment. They also offered 50 gold pieces."

Mary whistled, "Sounds like they really want this to happen. Fifty gold pieces could feed a poor family for life, or buy some top grade armor or weapons."

Within the magic community, there were several different councils and circles of magic. It was essentially a gathering of prideful casters who grouped together in an effort to display some form of authority. Besides the wizard council, there was also the circle of mages, the witch division, the technomancer court, the summoning council, and a few others. The groups were not limited to one nation or city, and many had small "guild" houses in every major population area. The wizard council was best known for their daring and insane magical experiments. Apparently, this time they wanted a slime removed from the dungeon intact for a pet binding. As dungeon monsters quickly evaporated outside the dungeon, this made it an impossible job already; not counting the low likelihood of success the actual ritual had.

"Well, thank you for your assistance Fiora." Mary smiled at her, "Your reward is downstairs with the ladies behind the desk. I'll let you know if anything else pops up."

Fiora got up and saluted with her good hand, "No problem Stormy," she winked at Mary, "I'm off to the local temple to get healed, and then I'm thinking of going into the dungeon again. I haven't had this much fun in a while."

As she shut the door behind her, Mary couldn't help but roll her eyes. "Adventurers, the whole lot of them are insane." She smiled, returning to her reports, "I really miss that life."

***

"Claire, how are you feeling?" Doc asked the little pixie. Claire had recovered from the backlash of the magic, but it had left her weak and house-bound. The pixie smiled at Doc's voice.

"I'm doing much better, thank you Doc. How was the boss fight?"

"I almost got them this time," he said with a hint of pride, "I even managed to injure that crazy sword lady, but that annoying archer shot me too many times. I managed to figure out how to move my body to dodge sword attacks, but magic and arrows are still my nemesis."

Claire giggled at him, "It's amazing how even in defeat you find the bright sides of things. Besides, magic and arrows can't be your nemesis; only people can be your nemesis."

Doc mentally shrugged, "It would be boring if there wasn't any challenge, and I can have any nemesis I want. Besides, I have fun against that group and look forward to their return." That particular adventurer team had come in a few times, but only made it to the boss room twice. They hadn't been within when he had sung, but Doc had picked up on their conversations about it. He thought it was funny everyone kept talking about it.

Claire dragged herself up into a sitting position, "As long as you're having fun, I guess that's okay. I still don't like hearing that you lost though." She frowned, "It's a matter of pride you know; my dungeon has to be the strongest."

Doc chuckled, "Whatever you say dear. Just lie back down and let me take care of you."

Claire blushed and covered herself with her blanket. He heard a muffled sound of embarrassment, but chose to ignore it. "Are your memories starting to come together?"

"They seem to be fixed for the most part," she said from under the blanket, "The main things I'm starting to see are differences in my lessons about dungeons. The memories affected were my perceptions of dungeons and the memories associated with them, like how dungeons differ by personality or environment. I can give you a little more knowledge now about other dungeons."

"I'm curious and listening," Doc announced, "However, please move the blanket down so I can hear you."

"You can hear me just fine in your mind," she complained, but lowered the blanket to reveal red ears, "Anyway, you're pretty rare for a dungeon. As I said before, an old soul like you doesn't often enter a dungeon heart crystal. In fact, it's one of those "once in a many thousand years" kind of deal. Mommy told me once that her great, great, great, grandfather was bonded to one and that it was a source of great pride for our family."

"Why would that be something to take pride in?"

"Because," Claire explained, "Most dungeons are soulless monsters, and I mean that literally. According to legend, the first dungeons appeared after some great, ancient war. Some say they formed from the blood and magic of their fallen bodies, but I digress. In places of high mana concentration, crystals tend to form within the ground. Sometimes, a formed crystal will form with the ability to absorb and control mana. This is a mana crystal, and is commonly mined for magical equipment used by the sentient races. A dungeon heart crystal is essentially a variant of a mana crystal because it also has the ability to "corrupt" the area around it."

"So, dungeons are evil things?" Doc was a little sad to hear that.

"No!" Claire shouted, "I'm sorry you misunderstood. Corrupt is the easiest way of describing it, but essentially the crystal can change the mana within itself and spread it through an area.

Anything touched by the mana falls under the control of the crystal. Now, as you have experienced, your race can only grow from magical power. While mana can be taken in from the environment, all crystals have the innate desire to grow as fast as possible. I say "desire" loosely because a dungeon doesn't have sentience until a certain level of power. When it first forms, it's a crystal with a tendency; which is lower than an instinct. As it slowly spreads, a new dungeon will come across small living things. It will pick up that by killing them; it will gain magical power faster. This forms a higher tendency to actively lure living things into its territory. From practice, it will eventually pick up the best baits to attract the best sources of mana."

Doc was intrigued, "So essentially, it's a slow transformation from being inanimate to sentient. That's rather fascinating; from non-living, to tendency, to instinct, to nature, and finally sentience."

"Yes, but it also doesn't help the dungeon be a good person. Dungeons are naturally selfish; it is the core of their being as they have no soul. Every living thing exists to increase a dungeon's power in their 'mind', but the older the dungeon the more cunning it is in regards to that. You are different because you've experienced life before somehow, which affected your development."

"So am I a good dungeon?"

"The goodest!" Claire agreed.

"That's not a real word."

"Stupid Doc needs to be quiet and say thank you for the compliment."

"Thank you, Claire." Doc deadpanned, "Can you explain the dungeon pixie role in all this?"

Claire nodded, "I think I can. Back near the beginning of dungeons, a forest pixie made a contract with one of the first dungeons. This dungeon was the oldest at the time, and thus was the craftiest. At the time, the pixie was fleeing hunters and took shelter within the dungeon. The pixie made contact with the dungeon heart itself after the hunters chased it down to the boss room. While the boss fought the hunters, the pixie made the first pack with a dungeon. In agreeing to bind his soul to the dungeon, the dungeon would protect the pixie forever. The pixie lost his green color and became black, and the dungeon achieved the first sentience level."

"Sentience level, what is that?"

"Basically, it began to refer to itself. Having the ability to call one 'I' is a big deal you know; it means one can refer to himself and thus can begin to learn how to grow as a person/monster. Anyway, the pixie had children within the dungeon, but the natural corruptive nature of dungeon mana passed the contract down to the children. They naturally sought out other dungeons and bonded with them, and their children also did the same. Over generations, the race of dungeon pixies came about."

"How is a dungeon pixie different from a regular pixie?"

Claire hummed for a moment, "Well, besides the connection with dungeons, dungeon pixies are only slightly different from our surface brethren. They tend to rely on wind or plant magic, but dungeon pixies are more naturally attuned to earth magic. Our colors differ as well; they being green, blue, or yellow while we are brown, black, or purple. Color can be random, though, so we don't rely on it too much. Dungeon pixies lost the ability to use healing magic, but gained the ability to control pure mana by forming things with it."

"Oh, so you mean those blue walls things with words?"

"Exactly it Doc," Claire nodded, "The most important thing a dungeon pixie does is pass down knowledge. Dungeons don't communicate well with each other; in fact, most tend to fight when they meet another dungeon. I'll explain how that happens in a moment. Dungeon pixies are taught from birth all about what a dungeon can do in order to keep dungeons successful. A successful dungeon means my race has a safe home and can flourish. Dungeons are rare enough these days because of incompetence or lack of knowledge, so this is really important."

Claire giggled as she read Doc's feelings, "You want me to explain about dungeons meeting each other don't you?"

"Yes, please; that sounds really important."

"Well," she began, "There are three ways dungeons can meet each other. The first way is natural, when two territories expand and touch each other. It tends to happen in places where there are more dungeons than usual. Typically, they each open up a hole and attack each other with their monsters. Since they are both dungeons, the monsters won't die when they leave their own dungeon. The winner eats the power of the other, killing the dungeon. Luckily for us, the dungeon pixie pact just moves over, so we don't have to die. In fact, we tend to gather and eat a meal while watching the battle."

"The second way is more mysterious." She waved her hands in an attempt to be spooky, but it only made Doc laugh. Disappointed, she continued, "Some dungeons gain the rare 'phantom ability'. It allows them to teleport temporarily to another location during the full moon. The adventurers think the dungeon is only open on the full moon, hence the 'phantom dungeon' name, when actually the dungeon just moves locations. If it meets another dungeon, they fight the same way, but with a time limit. When the night ends, the dungeon returns to its original location."

"The third way is the hardest way. Some powerful dungeons gain the ability to turn themselves into a floating island. They fly around the world in set patterns and encourage flying birds to nest on them. Adventurers use the beasts to get up to the dungeon, and most islands have a thriving town on them based around the dungeon. Island dungeons never fight each other because the effort would result in both dropping to the ground. They can fight ground dungeons, though, by settling down on the ground. It's a rare thing, but it has happened before."

"Do you think I could become a flying dungeon?" Doc asked.

Claire hesitated, then answered, "It's possible, but unlikely. Those dungeons tend to have an affinity toward wind magic, but not all of them do. Phantom dungeons tend to have shadow magic, but again it's not a strict requirement. That's something to wait for another day. For now, just concentrate on reaching the next level for more power. There may be others ways I'm not aware of as well."

"What about dungeon personalities; you said you remembered differences?" Doc prompted her.

"Not all dungeons are the same, just like every other living thing in the world." Claire began, "Some dungeons, like my mom's, are very selfish and don't allow big pixie families by eating any that leave the safety of home. Other dungeons encourage big families so the pixies can help manage the dungeon."

"So the personalities only differ when it comes to pixies?"

"Yup, all dungeons eat everything else. Well, many do accept monsters from outside, but have a strict power requirement."

"Okay, Claire. Oh! Another group is coming our way, wish me luck."

"Good luck!" Claire smiled at him as he left for his slime body. Claire pulled the covers up to her mouth as she stared down.

"Thank you Doc," She whispered, "But I won't tell you about... babies yet." She blushed bright red and covered herself with her blanket again.

Some things were meant for later.

Chapter 16

Simon the Shepherd sighed as he led his flock back to the barn. It had been a long day out in the fields; a very boring day for the young sheepherder. He had followed the flock of people out to the dungeon camp and watched it quickly change into a small town. The town had grown, but he was still a poor shepherd with only a few silver coins to his name from his momma.

"Get you sheep, come on now!" He called out, using his stick to guide the cackling creatures into their pen. He had hoped that he would be able to enter the dungeon for quick money, but had been disappointed to hear that the slimes required magic to kill. Even a cheap copper sword cost a lot of coins to be enchanted, so he was out of luck.

"Stupid dungeon," he muttered to himself as he locked the gate, "Why couldn't it have held goblins or animals? Why did it have to be so difficult and choose stupid slimes?" The boy was also a tad bit on the negative side, more likely to blame everything, but himself, for his problems.

As he closed the door to the barn, he walked over to the owner's house and knocked on the door. A butler walked out and bowed to him. "Fine job as always sir shepherd and a thank-you for your assistance," he said, "The master wishes you a good night. Here is your daily pay." He handed over a silver piece and disappeared back into the house.

Simon snorted, "Yeah, right; I bet the 'master' doesn't even know my name. Prick!" To be fair, the merchant who owned the sheep had a lot of business interests to attend to, but Simon didn't care.

What he did care about was getting home quickly. He rented one of the small tents at the edge of the town, and all the tents were magically protected. The other shepherds had been talking about wolves moving in the area, and one had commented on the rumor of a demon in the area.

"Not for me, nope, not at all," Simon muttered as he hurried away, "Only heroes are good for fighting monsters and demons. Leave the scraps for us needy people."

As he neared the town, a low growl alerted him to his surroundings. Cold sweat began forming on his brows as he slowly turned to his right. A pair of red eyes gazed at him, and was quickly joined by a low growl. His mouth dry, Simon slowly turned his eyes toward the town. It was close, but not close enough to escape if it gave chase immediately.

Thinking he was clever, he bent down and picked up a stick. He waved it at the eyes, "Doggy want a stick?" Simon had never seen a wolf, but surely it was just like a dog; he had never, however, heard of a wolf with red eyes. After all, only monsters and demons had red eyes because of all the blood they ate from virgins and tiny babies. As he considered this, the stick was torn out of his hand and he was knocked into the air. He flew and landed farther down the path, gasping for air.

Panicked, he struggled to his feet and hobbled as fast as he could toward the town.

"HELP ME! HELP ME, PLEASE!" He cried out at the top of his voice. He saw guards turn toward him and he felt relief flood through him. He was going to make it; he was going to live!

As if saying, "Nope," his leg was grabbed by sharp teeth and yanked back. He fell on his face with a cry as he screamed in pain. Needle sharp daggers cut through him and filled his mind with pain. The sudden rush jolted his mind, causing him to remember the stories his momma used to tell him; stories of demon wolves who stole through the night.

"Worgs," he whispered through the pain, "The demon wolves are here." He saw guards running toward him, but the beast pulled him away screaming into the night.

When the guards reached the spot, all that was left was blood filling small lines the size of fingers in the ground.

The night had come to life.

***

The night found Doc once again practicing his tentacle technique in the boss room. After days of hard work and practice, he had the focus and skill to control four tentacles at the same time. While on mana it may not have sounded too impressive, but considering the first boss fight that had involved no tentacles, Doc considered himself well on his way to tentacle supremacy.

"Great job and all Doc," Claire commented from above him, "But don't get too difficult. Killing everyone who challenges you may be good in the short run, but I guarantee that if you draw in the A rankers this early you will mostly likely die. I mean that in the permanent definition."

"I know Claire," Doc agreed, "But, I still think it's important to improve my skills. I want to get big enough to have multiple floors with a boss on each one. Can I be really strong on the final floor in that case?"

Claire giggled, "Of course, silly; feel free to go wild once you have floor bosses. Too bad you lack the variety for them as well as the space."

"A dungeon can dream, right?"

"Technically no, dungeons don't sleep and thus cannot dream, but I see your point." Claire rolled her eyes at Doc's annoyance, "Come on big boy, don't get your tentacles in a twist."

"That's a really dumb saying," Doc complained, "Twisting tentacles just fuses them together into a bigger tentacle. I can easily undo or redo them in any way I want."

Claire didn't have a reasonable answer for that, but her need for satisfaction was quickly forgotten as the two picked up on a commotion outside the dungeon.

"Sounds like the adventurers are in a mood, don't they Claire?"

She nodded, "Something has them riled up. Did you do something weird again?"

"I'm telling you the song was unintentional, but the answer to your question is no. Let's go see what's going on."

The two moved up to the dungeon entrance and peeked out; Claire from her hole and Doc from himself. From what they could see, a rather large battle was taking place in the woods near the dungeon. Flashes of fire and magic occasionally lit up the sky, but the action was too far for Doc to see who was fighting.

"Claire, can you tell what's going on?" He asked her.

The pixie put her hands over her eyes and squinted as she gazed into the forest. "I see a lot of figures battling some kind of animal... make that animals," she finally let out, "I think those are adventurers and guards fighting, but what they are fighting is beyond my sight in this darkness."

They watched the lights as they lit up the night, and occasionally commented on a pretty burst or particularly loud battle cry.

"Whatever they're fighting, it sure is making a lot of fuss. I wonder what kind of monsters or beasts could manage this."

"Well, I'm not familiar with the area, but we did sense those wolves the other day," Claire commented as she thought back.

"Would those wolf things really be so difficult to fight?" Doc asked curiously.

"Well," Claire began, "Wolves are known for their speed and pack efficiency. Unless they were dire wolves, I don't think any strong adventurer would have any trouble. Wolves have sharp teeth and claws, but very little defense for combat."

As she talked, Doc picked up on something approaching the dungeon. Forgetting Claire, his awareness wandered to the farthest edge of his territory and focused on the approaching figure.

A creature approached him, one he was not familiar with. It walked on four legs, and was covered by hair similar to what humans and elves had on their head. Its nose and mouth were longer than both races, and its ears were on top of its head instead of on the side. Doc also noted that it had bright red eyes; something he had never seen before.

More importantly, he immediately picked up that the creature was in distress. It stumbled every few steps, and he could see wounds on its body. However, the creature did not deviate from its course toward his entrance, its eyes resolute and unwavering. It carried two furry things in its mouth, and he could pick up the faintest of whimpers from them.

"Is that a wolf?" He wondered to himself, "It seems like it is hurt." Feeling sorry for the creature, he sent a tendril of magic toward it in an effort to comfort it. Working with tentacles for so long had made forming things into tentacle forms natural for him. As the magic touched the wolf, it froze and jerkily moved its head up to look at where his mind was. Doc could see relief in the wolf's eyes.

"How strange," he thought, "I didn't think beasts could feel anything." Yet, he could clearly see the emotions within the wolf's gaze, as its steps quickened toward the dungeon entrance.

Doc moved back to Claire as she finished her long winded explanation on wolves. "Claire, we are about to have a visitor," he announced.

Startled, she turned to him questioningly. He gestured with his mind at the approaching wolf. Claire's eyes widened.

"Doc, that's a worg!" She cried out.

"What's a worg?"

"A worg is a demon wolf. It is a type of wolf that evolved into a monster. It's very rare in these parts because the elves kill anything demonic as soon as they find it. Outside the demon country, anything with demon tendencies is hunted." She shook her head, "We can't let it enter the dungeon."

"Why not?" Doc asked stubbornly.

"The church, remember? They are really opposed to demon things, and letting in that worg will just spell trouble for us."

"She's injured and carrying little worgs. I'm going to help her." Doc declared.

Claire moaned, but knew it was pointless to protest further. As the dungeon itself, Doc had final say on anything dungeon related. They stopped talking and watched the worg pattered up to the entrance. It stopped right at the edge and sat down on its haunches. It dropped both fur balls and wheezed loudly as it bled.

"Oh mighty dungeon, I beseech thee for thy mercy." Doc and Claire heard a new voice in their mind.

"In return for thy protection, I offer my life and that of my daughters to serve you for the rest of our days. I swear on my heart we mean no harm to you."

"She's invoking dungeon magic." Claire quickly explained, "Remember how I explained to you what natural born monsters and dungeon born monsters were? A natural born monster can offer their monster heart to a dungeon, which binds them forever. They will not die within the dungeon, but become servants forever to the dungeon lord."

"So, I can make them monsters of my dungeon by accepting?"

"Yes, but I don't believe she's offering that of herself," Claire deduced as she eyed the worg's injuries, "She's dying, and so has offered her essence to you to increase your capacity. Her offspring, however, would become monsters for you to use."

"Oh mighty dungeon, do you accept my plea?" The worg asked again.

"I do." Doc answered simply.

The worg made a canine smile, and nudged its daughters into the dungeon. The fur-balls whined and licked their mother's injuries, but the worg pushed them away.

"Hush yourselves children. Serve this dungeon well for your family, as we entrust all our hope with you. Fare thee well, my children." With a last smile, the worg looked directly at Doc.

"Thank you," she said as she lay down and dissolved into a million small lights. The little worgs cried and pawed at where their mother disappeared, but she was gone.

"Claire, hurry and take them to the boss room." Doc ordered as he observed the forest, "I think those adventurers just finished their fighting."

The two of them tried to move the puppies, but the little ones were too overcome with grief and weakness to move. Doc noticed a few adventurer groups heading their way, so he forcefully took some slimes and had them carry the little ones away.

He watched the adventurers walk up to the entrance, and listened to them argue about whether to give chase or not. Feeling a bit annoyed, Doc used a tiny bit of magic to form a skull in the likeness of the worg mother. He had the skull grow out of the entrance wall and felt a certain sadistic joy as the adventurers jumped at the skull's sudden appearance. They grew pale and fled the area to Doc's immediate relief. Sighing to himself, he returned to his room, curious as to what he was to do with his new charges.

Chapter 17

The two 'pups,' as Claire called them, were deposited on the floor of the boss room gently. They huddled together and stared wide eyed at the overslime and dungeon pixie, whimpering and shaking. They were rather adorable in this position, especially with the dark red eyes that seemed to glow in the lowly lit room.

Doc scratched his body with a tentacle, "Claire, what do I do now?"

The little pixie flew down and landed in front of the puppies. Focusing her magic, her form grew to their size and she gently patted their heads with her hands. The puppies flinched at her touch, but eventually relaxed as they sensed her motherly intentions. With a whine, they dug their heads into her body in an attempt to seek as much comfort as possible.

"Didn't you say wolves bothered you?" Doc checked.

Claire shook her head, "These are worgs; they are not wolves or wargs. Also, these are babies and are so cute!" She hugged the puppies and gave a girlish squeal as their soft fur tickled her nose. "Worgs are wolves that evolved into monsters. They gained intelligence and nobility in their actions, unlike wolves who toy with their prey. Wargs are monsters that resemble wolves and worgs, but are completely demonic in origin and related to hell hounds and other creatures like them. I only told you worgs were slightly demonic because that's how the church views them."

The two had lived together long enough that Claire knew to answer his questions before he asked. Doc shrugged, "Good to know. Again, what do we do with them?"

Claire raised her eyebrow at him, "You're the one who decided to adopt them into your dungeon; don't tell me you didn't carefully consider what was going to happen."

"I prefer your giggling personality." Doc deadpanned.

"I prefer not having headaches that prevent me from giggling," she shot back, "But we have to make the best with what we have." She sighed and rubbed the heads of the puppies, "Well, at the very least, this is a good opportunity to teach you about another way of improving your dungeon: Monster Adoption."

Claire waved her finger as a blue screen appeared on the wall. It flowed with images that seemed to have been painted by a young child.

"Your skill with art is amazing as usual."

"No need to be rude Doc."

"What are you talking about? That's the best art I've seen," Doc said honestly.

"It's the only art you've ever seen," Claire muttered, but blushed all the same as she began her presentation.

She brought up a picture of two slimes, "As I've told you before, there are two types of monster in the world; natural and dungeon-born. Dungeon born monsters are created within a dungeon and are not truly alive, while natural monsters are born in the outside world and are alive."

She switched the picture to one of the wolves with an arrow pointing from it to a hole, "Now, sometimes natural monsters will go to a dungeon. Reasons aside, the monster will often do one of two things, either conquer the dungeon or join up with the dungeon. A powerful enough monster will devour any dungeon's heart it come across to increase its own power, which is why many dungeons try to have good relations with adventurers. The adventurers detour most monsters from attempting to do this."

"Now," she pointed at the picture, "When a monster decides to join a dungeon, it will offer up its monster heart, or core, if you prefer. The heart will then dissolve into magic power that the dungeon heart absorbs. The monster then would normally die after the loss of its heart, but instead it is filled with the dungeon's mana, transforming it into a dungeon monster with a soul-connection with the dungeon. Most boss type monsters besides the dungeon boss are of this sub-type."

"So these two can become bosses?" Doc asked excitedly.

Claire frowned, "Normally yes, but you accepted their mother's bargain. She offered her own heart for their protection, and her body was too weak to become a dungeon monster. Basically, you took her heart as payment to be their guardian. Since you accepted her offer, you cannot force them to become bosses without their consent."

"Okay, I can live with that," Doc said after some thought, "I don't believe in little ones killing to live anyway."

Claire nodded, "I thought as much, especially with your adversity toward the other matter. Anyway, the only thing we can do now is wait till they can speak and negotiate with them."

"We... can speak." The two heard a new voice in their conversation. Surprised, the two looked down at the two puppies, who were trying to sit as calmly as possible. Legs shaking, they locked eyes onto Claire and spoke slowly with purpose using the dungeon connection to link their minds.

"We... are young, but... we learned from our... mother." The two spoke together in unison, "We hid... this because we wanted... to see what kind... you were."

Claire stared at them, her hands twitching as she controlled her cuteness reflex, "You wanted to see what kind of dungeon Doc was before you spoke?"

They nodded, "Our… pack knew the dungeon… Doc was strange from… listening to humans. We were… on our way here when humans… attacked."

"Did you provoke them?" Claire asked gently.

They growled and snarled, "No! Stupid humans, we hate them! We no attack them! But," they hesitated and calmed down quickly, "We smelled another leading the humans… it smelled not human… like brimstone. It told… humans to attack… us."

Claire frowned as this, "In other words, the humans were led to believe your pack was a danger and attacked. This sounds like something a demon would do, and only demon-kin smell of brimstone."

"So demons are bad?" Doc asked curiously.

"Demons by nature are selfish and self-serving, but not all are like that." Claire explained, "The word 'demon' actually refers to great many monster types with an infernal origin, in other words, from an alternate dimension opposite to that of the divine realms. There is actually a demon sentient race that is tolerated by the others, and they are not evil. However, most of the monsters are and love to spread chaos. The imp race is an example, one that you could have chosen as a starter race."

Doc nodded and turned to the cubs, "Where did your pack hear of me? Why did they come when they heard I was strange?"

The cubs nodded, "Our pack understands human and elf and other races. We... know of strange dungeons by... tales of elves. Our pack... hunted everywhere and... needed home. Come... here for home. But," The cubs began to cry again, "Pack gone, no more pack. Momma, Momma gone!" Their wails filled the cavern and wrung the hearts of Claire and Doc in sympathy.

Claire flung herself into the cubs and hugged their crying faces into her bosom. "It's alright little one, it will be okay," she assured them with tears in her eyes, "I'll be your new mother and Doc will be your father."

"Momma!" The puppies cried out as they dug themselves into her warm affection.

Doc, once again, was thrown in intense confusion. "Err, what? Claire, I don't think this is going to work" Doc protested.

"Poppa?" The cubs turned to him with their wide, red, tearful eyes.

"Poppa is here!" Doc never had a chance against them.

***

After a massive slime hug, the four grouped together as Claire straightened her dress. "Now, all we have to do is finalize the formal agreement to our mutual satisfaction." Seeing the faces of the other three made her giggle, "I mean we have to make the cubs dungeon monsters and see what demands they have."

The cubs shared a look before facing Claire and Doc, "Can you remake... pack?"

Claire shook her head sadly, "No, dungeons can only make monsters in the evolutionary tree of their starter monster. Even if we could, they wouldn't be the same pack you remember."

The cubs nodded, sad but understanding, "We...understand. Momma joined with...you, so you are...also momma. We want... to fight humans and... we want to be part... of pack."

Claire nodded, "We can try to get some mimic slimes to copy you once they evolve. . . "

"Not new... pack; your pack." They explained, their tails slowly wagging behind them.

Claire paused, and then smiled at the little cubs. "We would be honored to accept you two into our family. I promise that we'll take good care of you in place of your mother." The puppies smiled and bowed their heads.

"We bind ourselves to you dungeon lord."

With that, the puppies were outlined in white light and blocked from Claire and Doc's view. Out of the light, two orbs floated out and dissolved into many small lights, which moved into the wall where Doc's heart was. As before, Doc felt his powers grow as the lights entered him.

The light dimmed down to reveal a surprising sight, two human girls.

"Claire, our new children have been kidnapped!" Doc cried out in alarm. He was slow to understand, but he was very dedicated to jumping on the bandwagon.

Claire was obviously startled, but she put a comforting hand on him, "Um, Doc, I think those are our children."

The two human girls uncurled to reveal some very non-human traits. Their ears were on top of their heads and furry and their faces were elongated.

Their bodies were covered in fur and their hands were padded. On their backs, a tail swished from side to side as the two smiled.

"Thank you for accepting us mother Claire and father Doc," the two announced together with a happy smile.

"Claire, please explain."

Claire twiddled her finger, "Um, well, I'm not positive about this, but I think they evolved from the experience. Worgs evolved from wolves, and I guess beast-kin are…"

"What are beast-kin?" Doc asked.

One of the puppies spoke up, "Father, beast-kin are one of the sentient races and descended from great beasts, magically changed humans and cursed beings. They look like hybrids of animals and people put together; however, we are not beast-kin." To demonstrate, the girl morphed into a large worg and gave them a toothy grin.

Her sister rubbed her ears and continued, "The dungeon did provide us the energy to evolve, but sentient races cannot bond to a dungeon. As a result, we took on the properties of your race and inherited the ability to change our form. Also, we absorbed enough knowledge to become adults." She fidgeted awkwardly and said to Doc, "We also know that you're male, so..."

"How wonderful!" Claire said loudly, "Can you become pixie size?"

The two paused, and then shrunk into small, furry winged pixie versions of their previous form. Doc couldn't hold back his chuckles as he turned into a puddle and began to earnestly laugh. Claire, on the other hand, was so excited she shrunk down and tackled the two into a hug.

"I have babies! So cute! I love you both already!" She cried out and flew them into her doorway, "Firstly though, we need some ground rules." They disappeared into the house as the door slammed, leaving behind an amused Doc.

"At least she's into it." He chuckled to himself.

***

In the end, the two new worgs were assigned as the new floor 1 boss. Thanks to the power boost Doc got from their mother and their hearts, he was able to add another room to the first floor specifically for them. He also was able to add a stairway and move his heart room down to the third floor. The overslime stayed on the second floor with the plant room, and Doc hid the stairwell behind a small wall. He couldn't actively separate his heart from the rest of the dungeon, but hiding it worked.

The two worg girls happily settled down as part of the "pack" and eagerly awaited the chance to battle adventurers. They were restricted to their worg form when adventurers were in the dungeon, but it was fine since that was the form they were most familiar with. Also, Doc and Claire had an aversion to their human-like form, so the girls promised to never transform without asking permission first.

***

Back at the camp, a dark figure stalked among the shadow and entered a tent. Closing the flap behind it, the form of Simon, the sheep herder, reached down and pulled a hidden bag of silver out from behind the cot. Smiling, Simon left his tent and walked into a guard. The guard turned and smiled at him.

"Hey, Simon, good to see you up and about again," he said happily, "Lucky we were able to save you from that worg."

Simon chuckled, "Thanks again for your help. I was wondering, where is the cheapest place to get a magic sword?"

The guard frowned at him, "You want to go dungeon diving? I advise against that Simon; it's dangerous; especially to someone unfamiliar with combat."

Simon waved away the guard's concerns, "Being helpless showed me how weak I am. I don't want to stay a weakling forever; I want to be a strong man for my family."

Moved, the guard smiled and handed Simon a note, "I understand completely young man. Here, take this note to the smithy down the road. The man owes me a favor, and I think he can help you with getting a sword. However, most likely you'll have to mine the copper yourself."

Simon smiled as he pocketed the note, "I'll be happy to do whatever it takes to grow stronger." His eyes glowed red for a moment in the torchlight, "Anything at all."

Chapter 18

The dungeon town was abuzz with activity after the previous day's events. Word spread quickly about the incursion of a pack of worgs and how they attacked shepherds on the road. They talked of the lone survivor who was barely saved by the town guard and how the adventurers had come together to eliminate the threat.

Above all, the loudest tavern talk clamored about the survivor worg. Two rangers had tracked a worg to the dungeon, but had been warned away by the skull of the worg at the entrance to the dungeon. Knowing the abilities of the dungeon, many now feared to enter and fight the worgs within. On the other hand, the knowledge of Moonglow now being present in the boss room had spread just as rapidly. Already there were guild requests for the flower, and the rewards for collection were some of the highest yet. The end result was that a community torn between fear and excitement, and the guards had to put down more fights during this day than any other.

The earth mage Rock sighed as he downed another drink. Rock knew his name was ironic for his occupation, yet that was how life turned out for him. His group had disbanded after their leader was killed during the worg battle, so now he was left with a few silver and nothing to do.

"Bartender, another round please!" He called out as he set his mug down. The older man behind the counter shook his head and thumped a mug of water in front of the mage.

"It's too early to get drunk fool wizard," he retorted, "Clear you head and go do something with yourself."

Rock shrugged and chugged the water in front of him. He wasn't the violent type, even when drunk, and understood what the man was telling him. A mage like himself was highly prized for battling slimes, even if his spells were limited to rock armor and a basic earth shot. He raised his mug of water and cried out, "To the best leader I've ever had; may his soul ascend gracefully into the heavens with a pint of ale and a heavily bosomed wench!"

The few patrons raised their glasses and cheered with him as they downed their glasses. Adventurer's tradition required the friends of the deceased to announce their death at taverns in order to honor their memory. It was a good excuse to drink, so the custom was very popular. Lady adventurers got the same treatment, though the words were different and more appropriate to their interests.

The young mage got up and tossed a silver piece at the barkeep; he caught it and chewed on it for a moment. Nodding, the man tossed Rock a few bronze in change and returned to polishing his mugs. Rock exited the tavern and made his way over to the guild hall.

The guildhall was designed to bring adventurers together. The floor was covered in tables and chairs where any could sit and seek others to join them. The massive board on the wall in the back was covered in requests that were separated into ranks, and a counter adjacent to it was staffed by members of the administration who checked the completeness of requests.

Rock settled himself down at an empty table and began to play with his rock. He levitated the stone in his hand and began to practice his control over it. As a mage, practice was very important and was encouraged whenever the opportunity presented itself. In the guild hall, however, practice also served to inform others about an individual's abilities.

It didn't take long for a warrior to stride up to Rock and examine him. "You are an earth mage," the warrior stated with a trace of arrogance. Rock nodded and had the rock move through the air. The warrior smirked at him, "It's your lucky day then mage, for my group has a need for one such as you. You should feel honored."

Rock suppressed the urge to roll his eyes at the warrior's attitude. It wasn't the first time he had had to deal with an arrogant man, and he could make it work as long as he was silent. Rock gave the warrior a small smile and said, "To whose honor am I delighted to make acquaintance with?"

The warrior, obviously a man of great wit and intelligence, paused for a moment as he processed the mage's words. Once he had, he smiled and held out his hand, "I am the mighty warrior Steinbeck, a rank C adventurer and third son of the House of Yaught."

Rock gave the man a flattering bow from his seated position. The house of Yaught was a minor nobility, but it was still well known for their control over some of the few mines near the city. Mines were rare in the plains and forest, so control over any mine granted power and influence. "It is an honor to meet you, Steinbeck of the House of

Yaught. I am Rock, a simple earth mage with experience with the dungeon."

"Rock," Steinbeck laughed, "What a silly name to have as an earth mage!" He clapped his hand on Rock's back, who braced himself from the man's strength. Recovering, Steinbeck straightened and held his hand out, "Feel free to call me Beck; it's what all my friends call me," he boasted, "Come, join my table and I'll introduce you to the other members."

Resigned, Rock got up and walked with Beck, the latter wrapping his arm around the former's shoulders and boasting of his many achievements in the field of battle. Rock smiled patiently, as he was genuinely interested in the man's stories. As a rank D adventurer himself, Rock was curious on how the loud and arrogant man had progressed so far to become rank C.

Before he could hear anything of interest, the two arrived at their table of destination. "Rock, allow me to introduce the other members of my party," Beck announced, "This is my girlfriend Milda; she is also a mage, but one that specializes in fire. The archer over there is Saran, and finally we have Michelle our resident healer."

Milda was quite the beauty in Rock's opinion. With a full bosom and long red hair under a wizard hat, she looked every bit the fire mage. She smiled coyly at Rock and unfolded her long, luscious legs. She refolded them as she watched his eyes wander down for a moment. With a subtle wink, she got up and began to fawn over Beck.

Saran nodded at Rock, then resumed a nervous twitching as he eyed the people around him. A thin, lanky fellow, he had short blond hair and his hand kept fidgeting toward his bow. He wore light leather armor and his boots shone with a hint of magic energy.

Michelle was a small blond haired girl. She bowed quickly to him and said, "Hello there, please call me Shelly." Her grin revealed a slight gap between her front teeth, which contributed to her childish charm. She wore robes of the clergy and held a staff in her right hand.

Rock bowed to the group, "Greetings to you all. I am Rock, an earth mage ranked D as an adventurer." Eyeing Milda, he turned to Beck, "Why do you need another mage? Wouldn't a speed warrior or thief be more appropriate to balance your group?"

As Beck opened his mouth, Milda interrupted him, "My wonderful man in his brilliance decided that we needed more power in our group. Seeing that a thief or speed warrior relies on weapons that grow increasingly difficult to fight slimes with, he moved to recruit another magic user to assist us. Naturally, we all agreed with him." Beck nodded with a grin, obviously pleased with all the compliments thrown his way.

Rock, on the other hand, was not amused. It was obvious that while arrogant, Beck himself wasn't that bad of a person. His girl, on the other hand, seemed very experienced with manipulating men and was obviously in love with control.

As Rock considered rejecting the offer, Shelly walked up to him and gave him a hug. "Mister is going to help us, right? We really, really need your help sir." She turned her head up and stared him in the eyes as her staff glowed faintly behind Rock.

Rock felt wonderful as he hugged the small girl in front of him. She was so adorable and cute, and he felt an intensive desire to protect her as a slight fog rolled over his mind. "Of course I'll help you Shelly," he declared, "I'll be sure to do whatever it takes to help you." Shelly's giggles made him happy and he began to laugh with her.

Milda gave him a smirk as she bent over to whisper into Beck's ear. Beck's eyes glazed slightly as he grinned. Rock was so happy and Beck felt happy too.

"Come on then," Beck said, hefting his sword, "Let's go to the dungeon!"

***

Rock rested as Beck cut through the last slime. They had just finished the third room of the first floor and successfully avoided the "pitfall path" as it had come to be known. There had been some ceiling ambushes, but Saran had pointed them out with his superior vision before they entered the room. Rock noticed the man was much calmer after the girls had talked to him.

He had made sure to stay away from both girls during the battle. As a result, his mental facilities were returning to him and he was slowly coming to terms with what had happened to him. The little sister was no healer; rather her abilities extended far beyond simple healing and encroached on powers the church frowned on. Indeed, the older girl, Milda, seemed to be more than a fire mage as well. From his observation, he would place them together as a family, except for their vast difference in appearance.

"If only I had paid more attention to wards," he muttered to himself, "I can't believe I ran across mind benders so far in the boonies." Mind benders were people with the ability to twist another person's mind. Not exactly mind control, it made the victims more agreeable and happy in the short term, but quickly caused an addiction that polluted the victim's abilities. It was not often used because of the notable signs, so the girls must have just arrived. Saran showed signs of at least two days of exposure, and Beck seemed to have been affected for about a day.

"Rocky, it's time to go!" Shelly called out to him. Rock pulled his fake smile and walked over to her.

"Okay, Shelly. I'm ready to go when you are."

She giggled and pulled him along as she skipped ahead. Beck, Milda, and Saran followed close behind; the two men held closely by the tall redhead.

As they walked down the corridor, Rock tried to remember more about mind benders. There was something specific that he needed to remember, something terribly important. His thoughts were lost as they came into a new room.

The room was the same size as the other rooms, the only difference being the staircase on the other side. As the party made their way across the room, growls echoed around them. From the shadows, two large worgs appeared on either side of the room. Their red eyes glowered as the new intruders came into their lair and slobber fell from their mouths.

Shelly's grip grew tight around Rock as she stared at the wolves. "Mr. Rock, were these monsters here before?"

Rock shook his head, "No, there has never been a floor boss for the first floor before. These must be the remnants of the worgs from the days before."

"Can we win Mr. Rock?"

He shrugged hopelessly and said, "I doubt it. Worgs are extremely fast and cunning, working well in groups. Our equipment was picked to battle slimes that move slowly, not these creatures." He surveyed the room, "It's unlikely that we will be able to escape without a fight though."

Michelle patted his arm and said, "Then, you'll do your best to make sure I escape, right? After all, it's important that I make it out alive."

Rock felt the fog returning as he smiled widely, "Of course Shelly, I'll be sure to protect you. Go along and run now." Rock heard Milda whispering similar things to the other men, who nodded and took battle positions with him. The girls began to inch toward the exit.

Seeing their prey leaving, the two worgs barked and ran at them. The girls screamed, prompting the men into action.

Beck roared out a battle cry as he leaped forward toward the worgs, swinging his sword out in a wide arc. Saran launched arrows at the monsters as he ran sideways. Rock chanted his magic and moved the power of the earth to shield Beck.

The worgs dodged the sword; one hopping over it as the other ducked under it. They both landed in front of a very surprised Beck and snarled at him. As he pulled his arm back, they sank their teeth into his arm and body, bypassing his leather armor and the small enchantment provided by Rock. Screaming, Beck turned and thrashed in a vain effort to escape his fate, but the worgs held on and began to whip their heads back and forth. Blood flew as they tore the flesh off his bones, his arm landing uselessly on the floor.

Saran launched more arrows and managed to hit the worg on Beck's arm. They hit and stuck the worg, but did very little damage and most bounced off the fur. Basic copper arrows lowly enchanted to deal with slimes had no effect on the beasts. It did, however, manage to get one's attention.

It whirled around and threw itself at the archer, who screamed as the man-sized hound landed its teeth first onto his legs. He screamed even louder as the beast whipped him across the floor and blood began pouring from his mouth. The beast finally let go and the archer went flying into the wall. He landed at an odd angle and moved no more.

In the meantime, the other worg finished dragging Beck's entrails across the floor. The man, barely alive, whimpered as his remaining hand tried to pull his guts back into his body. Coughing, he looked up in time to see the beast's jaws close around his head. Now, Beck was no more as well.

Rock at this point had backed all the way up to the wall. The fear and terror inspired by the battle finally succeeded in breaking the spell on his mind, but it was much too late for him. The exit tunnel was only a few feet away, but the second hound was already moving toward him from the same direction.

"So this is how it ends," Rock sighed sadly to himself, "Killed by the very worgs I hunted. I guess the irony is good enough;" He mused for a moment, before finally remembering what he needed to know.

Mind benders were extremely rare, because the ability was blood derived from an ancestor; one of non-human origin. In fact, the ability to cloud the minds of men had always been of that particular race's domain.

He slid to the floor and closed his eyes. In a moment, he felt a heavy wind on his face, smelling strongly of blood. He opened his eyes to see the open maw of the beast in front of him. Then Rock the mage thought no more.

Chapter 19

Doc winced as he watched his new daughters gnaw on the bones of his latest victims. While familiar with death, he actually had little experience with literal bloodshed as his slimes dissolved everything they killed. He wasn't squeamish, far from it, but it was still unnerving to see a man's pelvis being torn piece by piece apart; especially when the ones who were eating acted so cute to him.

"Are you having fun there girls?" Doc asked them. The girls had gone through 6 fights before adventurers had gotten wind of their existence and came better prepared. This latest group had managed to kill one of his daughters, but had still been slaughtered by the remaining one.

"We're fine Poppa," said the one chewing on a leg, "Dying hurt, but it was kind of fun coming back."

Doc had trouble talking to the two of them, as neither had opted to be named. They did everything together and often times answered together as well. "The Twins" had become their moniker, and Claire had agreed it was the best way to address them.

The pixie in question was currently watching the twins from a peephole in the walls, separating her tunnels from the rest of the dungeon.

"Girls, remember to wipe your mouths after chewing on bloody remains!" She called out, "While facing enemies with dried blood on your mouth is intimidating, it is also a sign of laziness and low intellect."

"Yes, Momma, we understand!" The twins called back happily.

Claire really seemed to be used to these kinds of things. Doc wasn't sure whether to be impressed, proud, or terrified.

The twins had successfully integrated themselves into the dungeon. Doc, whose consciousness was in multiple places at once, could hear the warnings being spread from adventurer to adventurer. He was proud of the fear in their voices; fear that was directed toward his dungeon. He also picked up that facing the two without a suitable reward would result in a bit infamy for his dungeon.

Specifically, he heard conversations in the copper room that went on like this:

"Did you hear about the new floor boss?"

"Yeah, I heard it was a pair of worgs; survivors of that worg pack a few days ago."

"No one has been able to get them yet, and a lot of adventurers are outraged at their presence."

"Why? It's not like there is anything good past them. The herbs are starting to lose their value anyway."

"You obviously haven't heard that Moonglow was round in the final room. The requests for the herb are staring to approach gold!"

"I doubt that, but a highly rare herb like that does sound good. I wonder what other plants will begin to grow in the future."

"Right? Now, imagine all those herbs, but the worgs are blocking access."

"So what; worgs are pushovers. My grandmother used to tell me how she killed worgs for fun."

"Bollocks to you grandmother; they are still killing people. I bet there isn't even a decent reward for killing them."

"Yeah, the dungeon loot is pretty low in value. I'll stick to copper thank you very much."

"I guess the loot is pretty bad," Doc admitted as he examined his slimes. The best loot was dropped by the grey slimes, but very few were ever killed and most were avoided as they primarily lived in the pitfall traps. "I wonder what I can do for rewarding the twin's killers."

The thought sounded morbid, but monsters who didn't die viewed death as more of an annoyance that an insult. Fighting also served as the main source of entertainment, so the adventurers were paying for rewards in their own way. To quote the twins on the subject of adventurers, "They pay with playtime or blood; either way we'll be satisfied."

Doc examined his astral bag. It was filled, but very far from being full; holding the equipment and weapons of slain adventurers as well as the small amount of coinage Claire had given him. He noted a piece of leather armor from his first kill, a robe from a mage, and even a potion. Muttering to himself, he turned his attention to Claire.

"Claire, I need help deciding what to give as a reward for fighting the twins."

Claire fluttered back to the plant room and settled down on her perch. "Do you mean the drop loot? That's easy silly," She giggled at him, "Just make it a part of them."

Not understanding her meaning, Doc raised an eyebrow at her--metaphorically speaking, of course.

"As you grow your dungeon repertoire," Claire explained, "You'll find that boss monsters are the easiest 'mob' to assign loot for; 'mob' being a shorter way of saying dungeon monster. Typically, a dungeon boss drops a piece of equipment that holds a small portion of their power within it. Also, the boss commonly drops better than normal equipment than the rest of the dungeon. For instance, a ring that boosts strength or swords of light are some examples for boss loot."

"How do I get that kind of loot?" Doc asked her, "That sounds like something rare that only good adventurers would drop."

Claire giggled again, "Silly, all you have to do is make it yourself. I realize our attention has been distracted by a great many things, but now it's time to work on the loot system for your dungeon."

The pixie flew to the wall and created a mana screen. She waved her hands and formed pictures of every monster type in his dungeon. "Let's change things up for everything while we're at it. Now Doc, how is the state of your astral bag?"

He shrugged, causing his slime body to jiggle, "It's got a lot of stuff in there, that's about it."

Claire nodded her head, "Great, now go ahead and dissolve everything."

Doc gave her a blank look. "Come again?"

"In order to create your own, unique loot, you have to understand both the type of equipment and the nature of the enchantment on it. As a dungeon being, anything you absorb into yourself is processed in a way that you know everything about it automatically. Dungeons are the only race in the land that can learn through absorption rather than active learning; another advantage you have over the other races. Dissolve everything in your astral bag for now."

Doc concentrated as his mana flowed through his astral bag. As it moved, his mana absorbed everything it touched and soon left the bag empty. He blinked as he felt things appearing in his head, things he hadn't known before, but knew now. "Claire, I know all about all these new things!" Doc cried out excitedly, "It's so amazing! I can see the ingredients for potions and the names of smithing techniques used to make swords!"

In his excitement, he flowed out and back into the overslime and began waving a multitude of small tentacles in every direction. Claire laughed and flew down to join him, dancing with the tentacles on top of his body. She swayed back and forth in time to the inaudible rhythm, her eyes smoldering as she took a tentacle by the hand and shook with it. Doc laughed and had the tentacle swing her in a circle.

When the moment was done, Claire flopped on top of his body and sighed as the overslime conformed to her shape. "Now that your 'knowledge dance' is over, it's time to work. Have you been making more silver and gold?"

Thinking of the gold and silver growing behind his walls, Doc nodded in agreement.

"Perfect, but we'll get to that in a moment. First thing is first, we need to make monster specific equipment. Things that hold a monster's power are quite rare, so it should appear once every 1000th kill. For your basic slime, try to make a belt."

Doc had lots of belts in his mind: thick belts, skinny belts, big belts, little belts, and even some decorative belts. He focused on one of the simpler belts in his mind, bringing it up and examining it with his mind's eye. A simple piece of leather, it was held together by a small oval buckle and could be sized for any body size.

With a shine, the belt materialized in the room. Claire inspected it as it fell to the ground and nodded her approval.

"This is definitely a normal belt, good job Doc." Claire changed the picture to one of a belt with sparkles around it, "Now, try to imbue this belt with mana. While you're doing that, imagine the monster who will have this and imbue their essence into it."

Thinking of his first monster, Doc thought of how they wobbled and crawled on the ground; how their bodies bent around obstacles and weapons. His purple light slowly seeped down into the belt as it glowed for a moment before settling back down.

"A belt that increases one's reflexes and agility; quite appropriate for a rare slime drop and a job well done." Claire complemented. "Now," She continued, "Try think of a weapon for the twins; something that relates to what they are."

Doc knew of just the thing, and focused himself. With another bright light, a pair of ornate, black daggers appeared in the room. The daggers were long and sharp, with a pointed guard and round pommel ends. A wolf head growled out from the bottom of the blade on both sides, and the entire weapon oozed blackness.

"Darkness attributes daggers," Claire said as she examined the pair, "How appropriate for our girls. These will be valuable to any who rely on the shadows to attack. I'm very impressed with how you formed this Doc; it shows you have a great imagination."

Doc blushed as his overslime body gained a tinge of red.

"Now's not the time for rest though; hurry and make more unique loot!"

When he was done, Doc had created a variety of equipment for his four remaining monsters: a minor healing potion for the herb slimes, a full leather outfit enchanted for physical resistance for the grey slimes, a magical hat that changed hair color for the mimic slimes, and finally a purple whip for his overslime. The whip had the added enchantment of inflicting minor acidic damage with every blow and could leave a serious burn on any who felt its touch. He separated the outfit for the grey slimes into its individual pieces, requiring multiple kills to get the whole set. Of course, every unique drop was extremely hard to come across, which made the outfit even more valuable.

Besides the unique loot, Claire also had Doc improve the general loot for everything. Monsters were more likely to drop silver coins with bronze coins, and the boss monsters had a rare chance of dropping a gold coin. In addition, all monsters had a small chance of dropping enchanted rings, whose effect ranged from minor improvements to a small boost in an attribute.

The herb slimes were also given an increased chance of dropping some of the herbs they had eaten, and mimic slimes could sometimes drop a vial of perfume. The perfume was a bit of humor on Doc's part, as he felt the human girls had a strange infatuation with smells and looks.

The entire process had required a lot of energy on his part, so when he was done Claire and the twins wished him a goodnight as he left the overslime on auto-pilot and flowed into Claire's bed. He relaxed comfortably as he went to sleep after a hard day's work.

Chapter 20
City State Duran

King Duran rubbed his head as he listened to the nobles in front of him arguing. As soon as word of the situation at the dungeon town reached the city, the noble party had been immediately called together for a vote on the matter. The issue at hand had been the rumors of malicious forces at work in the area. With the confirmation of the presence of worgs and rumors of evil demons roaming that area, the vote had been brought up to destroy the dungeon or allow for its continued existence.

"Order, I will have order in the room!" He called out, banging a wooden mallet on the table. The heads of the ten major noble families and their aides had gathered around the oaken table, and they quieted down as the orators of the debate stood up.

Father Tobias strolled to the front of the room, his robes lightly gliding across the floor. He faced the nobles and bowed deeply to them. "Good day to you, men of noble blood." He began, "I wish it was under better circumstances that we could meet."

He cleared his throat and held his hands out, "It is my unfortunate duty to bring to bare the issue of the day. In weeks past, the presence of the newly formed dungeon has brought much wealth to our fair city and your coffers." He waited through the mutterings of agreement, "In that time, the dungeon town has risen remarkably and become a special place for many interests. It is unfortunate, then, that the area has become a bastion of evil and corruption."

He held up his hands to quiet gasps and angry murmurs, "Thanks to the constant and consistent reports from the adventurer guilds, we know of the pack of worgs that was defeated some time ago. In addition, we now know that some of the pack survived and have become floor bosses within the dungeon. In addition to this, rumors have abounded the town of creatures of demonic origin in the area."

At this, the second orator stood up. Lord Mannis cleared his throat as he took a place next to Father Tobias. "Good father, while I agree that the surviving worgs are troublesome, it is not a cause for concern or worry. The dungeon has been confirmed to only hold the two worgs; which is hardly a cause for concern. In addition to that, many adventurers are praising the dungeon now for the vastly improved loot that has appeared in recent days. In regards to the rumors of demons," he waved his hand dismissively, "That is all they are at the moment, mere rumors spread by superstitious shepherds. There has been nothing to substantiate them and no reason to destroy a precious source of wealth." This set off another round of muttered comments of agreement.

Father Tobias raised an eyebrow, "So, you lack the faith to follow through on rumors of festering evil?"

Lord Mannis snorted at the veiled jab, "If evil truly was festering in the area, I would be calling for my troops at this very moment to eliminate the threat. Wargs, for instance, would have been a valid concern, while worgs on the other hand are merely stronger beasts and have no connection to any infernal origin. If this were truly a problem, the elves would have sent us notice and would have their hunters tracking the entire forest."

The good father smiled pleasantly and held his hands out, "What of the strange instances the reports have mentioned about people with their memories missing or the murders in the night?"

Lord Mannis scratched his chin, "It is sad when newcomers to the adventuring lifestyle drink so much they lose a hold of their head and wake up in barns with nary a stitch of clothing on their backs. In regards to the rumors, disagreements always arise when wealth is involved."

Father Tobias sighed and let his hands down, "I see there is little incentive for destroying the dungeon at this time. However, may I petition this council to allow for a bastion of faith to be established at the town? It would do well to alleviate some of the concerns that many followers have."

Lord Mannis smiled and bowed to him, "My dear Father, I will pay for the expenditures myself; no need to trouble the council on such trivial matters."

"Oh, ho, ho, how generous you are Lord Mannis."

"Indeed Father Tobias, I have often heard that word used to describe me." The two shared a laugh, though for some reason everyone else in the room felt chills down their back. Even in this council room, the two men held power that rivaled that of the king.

King Duran banged his mallet on the table, "In regard to the dungeon, the matter has been settled. Lord Mannis will finance the construction of a church at the town and Father Tobias will see to it that it is properly staffed and blessed for emergencies. All in favor?"

Fists thumped the table together, a sign of agreement from all present.

"Now, the next order of business is the war. Our latest reports..."

***

The Palace

Ken knocked on the door and waited.

"Come in." A voice called out.

He walked into the room of his sister, Princess Diana. The princess had made a complete recovery a few days ago, but the healers had denied visitors to her room until now. Ken had been waiting for his turn anxiously and had come as soon as his elder brothers and parents had finished their visit.

"How are you feeling Diana?" He asked kindly as he took her small hand in his.

Diana swatted his arm away and stretched her arms out from underneath her covers. She was wearing her normal clothes in her bed, a sure sign she was feeling better. "Dear brother, you know better than anyone that nothing could hold me down, not even death. Do not think I am some weak princess who becomes bedridden at the first sight of blood."

Chuckling, Ken walked over to her other side and sat on her bed. "You know, we were all really worried about you." He said, staring into her eyes seriously, "It was a very touch and go experience for awhile there. Even our elder brothers sat aside their feud to visit you."

Diana smiled and hugged her brother, "I know, and I am sorry for worrying you and everyone else. I truly regret it."

Ken smiled and returned her hug. When they were done, he cleared his throat, "I've been assigned by father to interview you on what you remember.

While I am sure he has already asked his own questions in front of mother, he wants to know if you can name any other members involved; also, he didn't want mother finding anything out, otherwise with her temperament she might blow up their entire families."

Diana giggled at the thought, and then frowned as she began to think, "My memories are not clear after I left for the camp. I have been trying to remember it myself, but there is a large gap between leaving Duran and entering the dungeon. I'm sorry I couldn't have been more help to you, but it is all a blur."

Ken smiled and ruffled her hair, "It's alright little soldier; we all know how traumatic that was for you. Tell me," he hesitated for a moment, "Do you suspect one of our family was involved in this atrocity?" His eyes were pleading as he held her attention on him.

Diana's face was completely neutral as she stared into the face of her big brother. "I don't know." She said honestly, "What I do know is that the seal was real, which means someone with great power or trickery used it or…"

Ken nodded, understanding her reluctance on the matter, for no one ever wanted to suspect family. "One last thing, can you describe this mysterious dungeon hero, Doc?"

Diana stared at him, "I can only say that he was noble and possessed good intentions toward me. It was too dark to make out his features, but I remember the strength in his arms as he carried me out of the dungeon."

Sighing, Ken smiled wryly as he patted her hair, "Thank you for your time, sister. I'll leave you now to your rest." They shared another hug and Ken left the room, filled with more questions than answers.

Diana waited until the door shut behind her brother. When she was sure he was gone, she began to shiver as she held herself. The fear had almost broken through her mask, but she had held it together. Every time one of her family came to check on her, she was overcome with fear and terror. Which one had been the one to target her? She had no idea, but with every hug given she searched for a dagger and with every smile given to her she searched for its falsehood.

"I'm not safe here," she thought to herself, pulling the covers over her head, "It's not safe for me here." She could feel the agony of terror eating her very existence from within, and that frightened her more than anything else. Not only was someone trying to kill her, she was also on the path to becoming a danger herself to everyone around her.

She knew the reason for that. Many thought of her as the muscle head of the family, but she had learned insight and cunning from her eldest brothers at a young age. "Those men were never out to kill me. Their role was merely to break me and turn me against my family." She had thought long and hard about what had happened to her, and she had lied to her brother about not remembering anything; she remembered everything and knew Sir Koran was involved. "If I hadn't taken steps to prevent this, I would have already fallen into the enemy's plans."

Indeed, she had been quite out of it during her rescue, but she had retained enough of her mind to put into action a plan to save herself. Thankfully, it had been a partial success; though it did contain an unexpected side effect. Her arm stopped shaking long enough to draw on her blanket, outing the fur in a circular pattern. "Mr. Slime, I want to see you again."

The Camp

Koran snarled as he threw his cup against his tent. The wine spilled as it tumbled and landed on the floor. "Explain this to me again," he growled, "What did my father say?"

The messenger cowered from the man's hostile gaze, "Your father bids you to not come home until this whole affair is forgotten about. He expects you to put on airs of generosity and to spread your good name through the area."

Koran groaned as he sat down onto his chair, folding his hands in front of his face. He was tired of hanging out in the boonies with weaklings; he wanted to return to the city and pickup wenches again. The only women out here were too dangerous to use and throw away; even the bar maids were protected by the male patrons and barkeep after hours.

His entire trip had gone to hell from start to finish. Exploring the dungeon had been interesting and all, but he had expected it to be an open and shut affair for a B-ranked adventurer like himself. Instead, he had received a letter from one of his partners in the city slums to wait there for a potential payday.

Koran had accepted the offer; he had no reason not to, and it gave him an excuse to woe Mary in the meantime. Sure, she was a filthy half-breed not fit to be in the same room as him, but Koran was taught from a young age to be a practical man by his father. Even half-breeds had their uses, especially the pretty ones as long as they were dealt with after. Koran relished for the day he could take her to one of the other cities with more suitable laws and have her sold to a brothel. He, of course, would be her first customer and he would get off on her begging and pleading for his love. After all, pleasure slaves were properly taught their proper place in life.

Unfortunately, he hadn't counted on the job to involve the princess. He had recognized her when she came in, but hadn't known at the time she was the target. That led to problems, such as the fact that she HAD SEEN HIS FACE. If she remembered, she could place him as the cause of the incident and ruin everything he had worked for.

The letter had outlined that the girl needed to be properly broken. It had even been signed by the royal seal, meaning he couldn't back out of the deal once he had read it; otherwise his life would have been on the line. Still, he had taken steps to make sure no one could place him at the scene. He entrusted the job to his most trustworthy "friends," the sons of lesser nobles who did whatever he wanted in order to gain prestige and influence.

Somehow, they had fumbled the job and completely ruined everything. They even had the audacity of dying before they could be suitably punished. Even worse, the princess had named them her attackers before passing out, which meant that eyes had turned a suspicious gaze onto him.

He cursed the mysterious dungeon savior Doc; cursed him for his interference in his affairs. Now, Koran was forced to play nice with weaklings in order to waive suspicion off of him, and now even his father was taking steps to distance him in case he was found guilty.

"Leave. Tell my father I will remain here to preserve my good name." Koran commanded, "But, be sure to remind him that if I go down, I'll make sure he comes with me." They had the perfect father-son relationship: practical, distant, and fully connected. The messenger bowed low as he hurried out of the tent.

Koran mused on his chair. In order to salvage his name, he needed to make generous gestures to the people. He was well versed in political maneuvering and knew how to play with lesser beings, but his mood wasn't up for it.

A knock at his tent distracted his thoughts. "Enter," he announced, "State your business."

A man walked into his tent and smiled at him. "I hear you have been busy," he said, a sinister undertone to his voice, "Since you've had such a hard time, I decided I would come help you."

Koran turned red with anger and stood up suddenly, "Who are you to..."

With a blink, the man held up Koran with one hand by the neck. Koran gasped and struggled, but found he could not escape the iron grip of the man in front of him.

"You know," the man mused, "While I should kill you for your failure, I really should be thanking you. I haven't had this much fun in a while; killing through proxy gets tiring after a few decades. While you delayed my plans, you didn't actually fail completely so I guess you can live for now." With a casual toss, he threw Koran across the room into his bags.

Koran gasped for air as he struggled to his feet. Casually, the man put his foot onto Koran's head, keeping him in a kneeling posture.

"Now, this is what's going to happen. You, in your generous spirit, are going to take a new adventurer under your wings and train him in the dungeon. You are going to help him with everything he needs, and then we are going to expand until you are teaching an entire class of new adventurers. Once your reputation has been restored, you will return to the city and help me deal with the royal guards for the next phase of my plan. Do you understand?"

"Yes, yes I do!" Koran cried out, "Please, tell me who you want trained and I'll do it!"

The man chuckled and removed his foot, "Why, me of course. I just recently registered as an F-ranked adventurer and I am in need of a mentor to teach me everything about dungeon diving. In fact, I think being taught how to kill a dungeon should be your last step."

Koran gasped, "If that happens, the whole town will fall into an uproar..."

"Yes, this will divert attention from the city. All according to plan, you see." The man chuckled, "Don't worry, you and your father will be suitably rewarded for your assistance, have no fear. In fact, here is a small incentive to help you."

A bag dropped in front of Koran's hands. His greedy eyes widened as the bag deposited its contents of gold across his floor. Koran gulped audibly, "What do I call my new apprentice?"

"Call me Simon." The body of Simon smiled evilly, "Just, Simon for now."

Chapter 21

Doc yawned as he watched another adventurer fall into a pitfall trap. He'd switched things up and put pitfalls next to aerial ambush holes, which tricked adventurers into looking up and walking around the holes and thus falling to their deaths. This time, it was a man in leather armor who cried out in fear as the grey slimes dissolved his body.

He switched over to check his magic capacity. Thanks to the new traps and the twins, his daily magic gain had increased to the next level. "Claire, I want to upgrade!"

On cue, his pixie companion flew out of her house and took her standard spot on her pedestal. "Oh, is it that time already?" She asked excitedly, "This is wonderful; it's my favorite part of the dungeon experience."

"Can we come and watch?" The twins asked them.

"You can come, but leave your bodies to their duties, okay my babies?"

"Yes ma'am." They chorused together.

An interesting fact that Doc learned was that like him, the twins could leave their bodies and let their minds travel the dungeon. They were limited to their room and his heart room, but it was still very impressive for a dungeon monster. According to Claire, the reason they could travel was because they had souls, even if they were dungeon monsters in actuality. Even if Doc lacked a soul, however, he would still be able to move everywhere because he was the dungeon itself.

Doc and Claire felt the twins arrive in the room like a gentle breeze. Formless, the two watched happily from the walls as Claire sat down to begin.

"Okay Doc, it's time once again to decide what you want to improve," she declared, waving her finger, "Do you remember your choices?"

Ability	Description
Teleporting Glyph	Inscribe a glyph on every floor that allows adventurers to move from one floor to another easily. Must have cleared the floor to be able to move to it. Groups are restricted to the lowest level conquered by a member
Additional Race	Able to create an additional race to the one held. Increases dungeon diversity
Upgrade Monsters II	Grants the ability to improve monsters by unlocking next evolution level.

	Current Monster levels: Slime Level 2
Instances (Acquired)	Able to create parallel realities within the dungeon, allowing for more adventurers to enter the dungeon at the same time
Environments	Able to create new obstacles in the form of environmental hazards.
Trap knowledge	Able to improve and add to existing traps by using mana. Current trap types available: pitfall, aerial. New trap types: launch, ceiling-fall

Mana Stones	Throughout the dungeon, places naturally fill with ambient mana. Now, those places will condense into mana stones that can be mined
Locked	Locked

"Claire, there are new options here." Doc said in surprise as he read through the options on the wall.

Claire giggled "Of course silly; as you grow stronger you'll gain more abilities as well. The options you receive in the future will depend on the abilities you chose now, so no dungeon is ever exactly the same." Claire stared at the mana screen for a moment, 'It seems that magic traps and mana stones are your newest options; most likely because of all the mana usage you've been doing lately.

Magic traps are the next step for you and will increase the lethality of your dungeon. On the other tentacle," She stared pointedly at his overslime form, "Mana stones will increase the economic value of your dungeon. Some of your monsters may start to drop them, and mages will flock here to acquire them. Since mages are your weakness that may be counter-productive."

"I really want to see more evolutions for my monsters, so I want the next evolution option." Doc declared. The twins mentally clapped at his declaration.

Claire held up a hand, "Before you leap into that option, hear me out. Your slimes are not done gaining new forms; there are many other forms your slimes can change into. Even then, since no dungeon has ever used slimes primarily, there are most likely slimes I've never heard of before as well."

Doc jiggled in agreement, "Well, what do you suggest then?"

Claire considered his question and tilted her head, "It all depends on what you can get your slimes to eat; that's the primary method of evolution for slimes."

Doc paused, "Do you mean the mana stones?"

Claire clapped her hands happily, "Your intuition is getting better every day! The answer is yes, the mana stone upgrade would definitely unlock the basic elemental slimes for you. Just imagine it: water, fire, earth, and air slimes all crawling around in your dungeon."

"I want it!" Doc cried out, "I want it!"

Both the twins and Claire giggled at his youthful exuberance.

"Poppa, you're really silly."

Claire added, "Yes, dear, calm yourself."

Doc turned completely red at the words, "Hey, you finally called me dear!"

Now it was Claire's turn to blush, "W… well we have kids now s… so it's appropriate." She twisted shyly, "Do you like it?"

"Of course!" The twins giggled and teased Claire as she hid her fiery red face in the plants.

Doc, not picking up on the situation, turned back to the screen. "Well, I don't need to increase lethality yet, so I guess that's a 'no' to traps and environment changes. The teleporting glyphs aren't necessary yet either and I have no desire for another monster race." Doc turned back to Claire, "Do I have enough capacity to get mana stones and the second evolution upgrade?"

He finally notice Claire's lack of presence, "Claire, where did you go?"

"Momma is taking a quick break Poppa, but she can hear you through us." The twins announced, "To answer your question, you can, but you won't be able to grow another floor for a long time. If you chose the Mana Stone option, you'll be able to grow two more floors. If you choose the next evolution upgrade, then you will only be able to create one new floor."

Doc frowned as he considered the options. His desire to grow outweighed his desire for evolution, so he needed to expand another floor.

"Wait, I already have a third floor." Doc realized with a jolt. Previously, he had separated his heart room from the final boss room and moved down a floor, hidden behind a secret wall. Wringing his tentacles together, Doc focused on his third floor.

It was just a single room, but his power had already permeated the entire level, enough for another floor set. "Okay, I'll get both upgrades!" Doc decided, "Time for more slimes!"

Instantly, he felt his capacity diminish as his mana was condensed into his crystal body. He felt it grow within his room as it again doubled in size to 4 inches. Doc, drained from the ordeal, smiled weakly as he inspected his body.

"Now, time to change up the dungeon!"

Focusing on himself, Doc inspected his current setup. The first floor was straight, holding the mining room and the boss room. The second floor winded around to the second boss room.

"This is boring now, let's change it up!"

Doc liked the first floor how it was, but he did move the twins from the first floor to the second floor. He moved his overslime from his final room up to the first floor boss.

"Poppa, why did you move us down?" The twins asked him curiously.

"You guys are really strong." Doc explained, "So I want adventurers to not be discouraged from exploring the rest of the dungeon. Besides, I want a new body."

Instead of a winding floor, Doc changed the second floor completely. He first made it like the first floor, a simple line, than added a few dead ends and paths that led back to the beginning of the floor. The original 5 rooms were still a part of the floor, but now there were more tunnels than rooms. The last room was, of course, the twin's room and held the staircase down to the third floor.

For the third floor, Doc improved upon his ideas for the previous floor and made it more of a maze style. The main path through the level held 3 Y-shaped tunnels that each held a false path back to the beginning of the floor. Also, he made sure the fake paths were littered with traps. The main path was actually quite short, reminiscent of the first floor, and led to the plant room.

***

"Poppa? Poppa!"

Doc finally came out of his building trance in a startled yelp. He turned and faced the twins, who were staring at him with worried eyes. "What is it girls?"

"You've been building for two whole days Poppa, and Momma has been sleeping the entire time."

"What! Is she alright? What about the adventurers, did they get hurt?"

"She's just sleeping; she's not hurt at all. The adventurers are okay as well. When you started working all the humans and elves were magically ejected from the dungeon. The entrance was blocked until you finished with the first floor, and then each subsequent floor was blocked until you finished with it."

Doc sighed out in relief; he hadn't wanted to kill all the adventurers so easily. It ruined the point of the whole dungeon experience and cut down on his entertainment.

"I'm glad, but I'm going to check on your mother now so return to your room girls." With a chorus of goodbye, he felt the twins move back to their room to wait for their next victim/playmate. Doc flowed into Claire's bed.

Her magic energy felt fine to him, so he formed a tentacle and tickled her nose. Claire sneezed cutely and yawned. She sat up and stretched out, smiling gently at Doc. "Good morning Doc, did you finish fixing your dungeon?"

"I did, but explain to me what happened to you. I was worried I messed up." Doc searched her body for any sign of damage.

Claire giggled, "Are you worried about me? While adorable, there is no need for that. When you undertake large projects, I'll naturally fall asleep until you finish up. It's a safety precaution for us as a species so we don't get caught up in accidents while the dungeon is moving things around. That being said, me falling asleep means that you've reached a sufficient stage of dungeon size, so congratulations."

Doc smiled happily, "Thanks Claire, I couldn't have done it without you. I have one last thing though; I need to make a new dungeon boss."

Claire nodded and she got out of bed. Doc appreciated her sleeping attire, which was basically the same as her normal clothed except for the long robes. "Give me a moment to dress and I'll join you in the plant room."

Shrugging, Doc obliged her and moved his awareness into the plant room. After a moment, Claire flew out in her normal outfit and settled on the floor.

"The first time you made a dungeon boss, you merely injected your essence into one of your minions. We will be doing the same thing this time, but with a higher evolved slime." Claire pointed at the ceiling, "Your old dungeon boss will always be the strongest version of its particular species of slime, but now that you're moving into a new boss body, other slimes will begin to evolve into overslimes by themselves. Of course, they will not be present on the first floor, only in the areas after the overslime boss."

"So, an overslime is one of the evolutions I unlocked?"

Claire shook her head, "No, an overslime is a 1st tier evolution; it was just locked until you made a new body. This process will repeat until you create a unique dungeon boss of your own. Moving on, let's get to evolving!"

Claire flew around the room rapidly, sprinkling the floor in pixie dust. When she was done, a glowing blue circle was left in the ground. "Summon the underling you want to evolve," she announced, "Remember, you can only use the monsters that have already evolved into your dungeon. You can wait for new evolutions, but this will leave you defenseless until you do."

Doc nodded, "I chose the herb slime."

Claire almost fell out of the air in surprise, "Really? Why that slime? I would have thought you would have picked the mimic slime or grey slime; both offer good boss forms and are well known."

Doc nodded in agreement, "Yes, that's it exactly. I want those two to evolve into new forms; not be locked while I play in my new body. I guess I could have picked the overslime again, but I wanted to try something different."

Claire giggled as she landed on her perch, "Well, if there is something I've learned it's to expect the unexpected with you. Go ahead and create your herb slime; I'm curious to see what it will become."

Concentrating, Doc used his mana to create an herb slime in the middle of the circle. The greenish-purple blob wobbled as it floated up from the floor, mindless and obedient. As with the original slime, Doc poured his essence and awareness into the slime. The slime wobbled and jiggled as it drank him in, changing forms as it grew.

When he was done, Doc and Claire stepped back, figuratively once again, to inspect their newest boss monster. The former herb slime was now slightly bigger than the overslime. It had grown spikes on its body and was pure green in color. Claire clapped happily as she inspected the slime.

"It's a jungle slime! I've never seen one before outside the southern jungle; how rare!" Claire gushed.

"You've been to the southern jungles?" Doc asked.

"Not really, but Mommy showed me pictures with her mind from her trip there. Dungeon pixies have a big meeting every fifty years to share dungeon knowledge. Our bodies stay in our homes, but we can magic our minds to meet at a pre-picked dungeon in astral form. I've never been to one before, but I heard they are really fun and the best places to find mates."

According to the blue magic screen, jungle slimes were a second tier slime found in warm, jungle environments. After absorbing enough earth mana and plant life, herb slimes could evolve into one as an option for their next evolution. Jungle slimes were naturally attuned to the earth, making them resistant to water and wind magic but weak to ice and fire magic.

Like their previous evolution, jungle slimes were capable of spitting a potent poison from their body and were now covered in poisonous spikes. Unlike their previous evolution, jungle slimes had a limited control over nearby plant life and could use them to capture their prey. However, this tendency to wrap prey had caused the decrease of speed for the entire species, resulting in some of the slowest members of the slime race. As like before, this jungle slime had a general element of magic due to Doc being its originator. The bonus was that, as a boss monster, this particular jungle slime had a far more potent poison than its lesser brethren.

"This is just what I need for the plant room." Doc said happily.

"I agree, it is the perfect choice for you." Claire declared as she floated down and sat on the slime.

She rested back against a spike and frowned, "I think I'll miss your old boss though; it was a much better seat than this."

As if hearing her, the jungle slime shot a spike into the ceiling, leaving a blank spot on its body. Claire happily lay on its back and sighed in contentment, "Never mind, this is perfect."

Chapter 22

A carriage pulled up to the adventurer's outpost. It was flanked by four guards on horseback. Mary stood at the entrance, waiting patiently for the occupant. She had received a letter a few days prior, and was well informed of her coming.

Princess Diana, in her normal warrior attire, walked out of the carriage and up to the vice-guild master. The two stared at each other for a moment - words being exchanged by their eyes - before the two rushed forward and embraced.

"It's good to see you again Mary," Diana said happily.

Mary, wiping away a tear, smiled gently at her, "I am pleased to see you safe and unharmed princess."

The two had met years earlier when Diana was just starting out her training as a young girl. Her father, thinking it was just a phase, had sought out

Mary's assistance as he feared a boy's harsh training regimen would be too intense for his little princess.

Mary, of course, thought the boy's course was too light and put the young girl through hell's personal slice of training. Diana complained and moaned, but she had persevered through the training to become one of the most promising rookies of her year. Mary had been there when the princess had graduated from basic training, beaming the entire time.

As they pulled apart, Mary turned to the guards. "Gentlemen, I will take over from here. Your first round at the tavern has already been covered, so have at it."

The guards clanked their swords together and bowed. After they left, Mary returned her attention to her protégé and close friend, "Come, we have much to discuss together. I want to hear about the incident directly from you."

Diana winced slightly, but put on her brave face and followed Mary up to her office. There, the two sat across one another; one brooding and the other sweating. With the guards gone and nothing to disturb them, Mary's face changed to one of extreme firmness.

"Explain." It was only one word, but Diana shivered from the aura that dripped from it. She had been dreading this meeting for quite some time, but compared to the terror she felt back at the palace, this was much more bearable.

"It began after third brother Ken returned from the dungeon inspection," she began. Diana described the conversations with Ken and her twin that had led to her coming to the town by herself. She described everything that happened in the camp, including Sir Koran's involvement; a fact that she had not told anyone else. She went into detail about the incident in the cave; how the men attempted to assault her, how she ran and fell, and how she could hear their terrified screams as she lost consciousness. She told Mary everything that happened to her, except, she did not tell her about Mr. Slime. She described the feeling of being carried to safety, but attributed it to the mysterious adventurer who had rescued her. She even went into detail about the fear that constantly plagued her at home.

The reason she trusted Mary went beyond the normal mentor bond; the two had sworn a blood oath together when Mary had graduated, one that connected them in a world that looked down on them for their gender or blood. Their bond was greater than family, for it in itself was its own form of family; a special type of blood bond. Mary's unique blood could tie her to those she truly cared about so she could always be aware of their condition. It was she who sent out the search parties for Diana when she had been hurt; otherwise no one would have known the princess was in trouble.

Mary rolled her fingers on her desk as she listened. Her eyes never left Diana's face as she considered every word. Finally, she sighed and leaned back into her chair. "What a mess you've dragged me into." She scratched her hair and sighed, "Why couldn't you make this any easier for me?"

Turning serious, Mary stared hard into Diana's eyes, "First thing, how could you let yourself be taken in by those fools' words? Remember what the first thing I taught you was? Failing to control your emotions is the first step to destruction. I can't believe one of my best students forgot such a crucial thing during her first real battle."

Diana winced, "I remember that now Mistress Mary, but I couldn't then. It…it was so scary." She shivered as the memories came back to her, "They had no hesitation, no remorse; just their lust and that letter of permission from my own family. Someone who has loved me my whole life wants me hurt, and I don't know who."

Mary sighed and walked around to hug the girl. "I understand girl, believe me I do; and so does every boy or girl who has ever had a first battle. I can only blame myself for this, for never giving you the chance to experience a life-or-death situation."

Diana, forgetting her fear for a moment, shot Mary an angry look, "What are you talking about? What about that time with the tree monsters?" She retorted angrily.

Mary waved her hand, "Irrelevant; you knew that was training for you. I mean, you've never fought life and death battles with other people, not monsters. It's even worse for women like us because of what a man can do after we're beaten." She clenched her fist involuntarily, "I'm sorry you had to go through that, especially with that atrocious letter. I cannot imagine the shock that gave you."

Diana hiccupped a tear as her shivers returned in Mary's embrace, "I'm really glad they didn't touch me, really I am. I don't know what I would have done..."

"You would have broken and splintered," Mary said flatly, releasing Diana and returning to her chair, "I've seen it before in men and women who lived through disaster and tragedy. Their gazes were empty and their hearts were filled with such negativity I thought they would drown from it all. I suspect, as you do, that your mentality was part of some greater plan, one that was foiled due to the adventurer Doc."

"Speaking of which," Mary cast a curious look at the princess, "How did you manage to preserve your sanity? I could tell from our hug that while hurt and completely terrified, you remain unbroken and, more surprisingly, not corrupted by anger or fear. In fact," Mary twiddled her thumbs in thought, "I could have sworn I sensed a strange calmness inside of you. What did you do to yourself to get like this?"

Diana blushed and shook her head, "I don't know what you mean."

Mary snorted, "My dear, your mind is shaken yet unbroken. Your body was hurt, but your soul remains pure. As one who was praised as a newborn to be a disciple of the gods, I cannot believe an experience like that could not change you. You remember being one, correct?"

In the many countries on the continent, there were many shrines, temples, churches, and cathedrals dedicated to the many gods of the pantheon. In rare cases, a child would be born that would be blessed by the gods and become a 'god's disciple.' These men and women would be masters of the portfolio of the god or goddess who blessed them. For instance, a man blessed by the god of swords would be a master swordsman or a woman blessed by the god of agriculture would be able to grow the most delicious crops in the kingdom. Being a disciple, however, carried its own risks. Until one's

20th birthday, when the patron god's blessing would become permanent, disciples could easily be influenced by other deities into switching sides. As a result, they tended to be emotionally sensitive and easily affected by their environments. Many of the so called 'Demon Kings' of the past who had threatened the world were actually fallen disciples who had been corrupted by dark gods and goddesses.

Diana nodded with eyes downcast, "I remember Mary; I never forgot my duties. But," She hesitated, "Ever since I went to the dungeon, I feel like I stabilized into my patron."

Mary hummed as she rubbed her eyes, "What you are saying should be an impossibility. No disciple has ever stabilized before the age of 20. The only way that would happen was if your heart and soul had settled on a deity. And yet," she muttered to herself, "Here you are, safe and sound, for the most part, with your mind stable and your soul pure. If what you say is true, then you have some special connection with a new god or goddess, and it is they who saved you somehow."

Diana looked down at her hands, "Well, if what I think happened for sure, then perhaps you are correct. I have a new patron."

Mary paused, then slammed her hands on the table, "Fool girl! Don't tell me that is what you did! You have no idea the personality of this new deity; have you lost your mind entrusting your soul to another…"

Diana stood up and stared Mary down with determination, "I know what I did and I have not regretted my decision. If anything else, that's the only reason why I'm here today talking with you."

Mary deflated back into her seat, "I have to agree, I most certainly have to agree with you on that point. Still, what you have done cannot be taken back. Are you prepared for the consequences?"

Diana folded her fists and nodded, "I've been prepared for a while now." Diana no longer shivered and her eyes shone with new resolve.

Mary nodded, "As expected of my apprentice. Now, we must plan for the future." She walked over to a cabinet and removed some paper. Returning to her desk, she dipped her pen and began writing.

"Now, if what you told me is true, you falling into an unstable state of mind was very important to whoever gave Koran that note. Since his involvement was made known to the gossip-mongers, he's been running back and forth trying to save his reputation. In fact, he's been doing some charity work for some of the new adventurers; taking them into the dungeon and showing them how to fight properly. I'm sending him a note asking him to take you on with his class."

Diana smiled, a hint of bloodthirstiness leaking out of her, "So I, the poor frightened princess, will beg the handsome adventurer to help me break my fear's hold over me; is that correct?"

Mary returned the evil smile, "Indeed, my young apprentice; so it's important we get you to join his class. Since your attack was misplayed, incidents have been occurring in and around town. I have a feeling our shadowy friend is keeping a close eye on his servant. By the way," Mary paused to look at Diana, "You haven't told your family about any of this?""

Diana shook her head, "I can't take the chance that one of them is involved, and I don't want the innocent members hurt in this affair."

"In other words, you want personal vengeance."

"Yes. This was an attack on me, and I must return the favor."

Mary chuckled, "I guess I taught that point a little too well. No matter, you will have vengeance." She folded the paper and slid it into a note tube for delivery.

"I'll see that Koran believes you don't remember anything and accepts you eagerly into your class. In the meantime, I'll invite some of my friends to join your group the same day you do as guest lecturers. Koran will see it as a chance for endorsement and will eagerly accept their help." Mary stood up and gazed out the window with her hands together behind her back.

"Everything will end in the dungeon, where it all started."

Chapter 23

Koran almost dropped the letter in excitement after the messenger left. The princess did not remember him, and she was even going to join his class tomorrow. Life was looking up for him again!

"Master, he said, turning to Simon, "This is wonderful news is it not?"

Simon smiled as he lazily raised a goblet into the air, "It is the best possible kind of news, servant. Now I can undo your mistake and make sure the girl is mine once and for all. If everything works well, I'll even have that other adventurer group as pawns for the next stage."

Koran was familiar with Lady Fiora's adventurer group. While a lower rank than him, Fiora was on the fast track to becoming B rank soon, and it bugged him to no end that not only was she better than him she also refuted him. Due to her connections, he had never pursued her, but if she became a pawn then his master would likely let him use her for his personal pleasure.

He licked his lips in anticipation. Years of experience had taught him the best ways to incite pain and pleasure in his companions, willing or not. In the end, he had learned all women would bow as long as he pressed the right buttons. Why, they often times took their own lives when he was done, which spared him the awkwardness of killing them after he was done.

"Silence your thoughts," Simon scolded, "I will personally cut your dick off and feed it to you if you let your lust cloud your judgment. Focus on the task at hand."

Koran winced and reflexively covered himself protectively, inciting a laugh from his master. Coughing, he asked, "How will you ensure they become your pawns, sir? I know not..."

"Of course you don't, you fool," Simon growled, causing the larger man to grovel, "All I need is a heart filled with despair or broken. My power flows through such things and, when I eat the heart of the dungeon, I will have the ability to take hearts of a purer nature. Eventually, all will fall to my power and you, my servant, will reap the rewards."

"Yes master, it is as you say."

"Just prepare for tomorrow; it is the future we aim for."

***

Diana checked her reflection in the magic mirror one more time. Her luscious hair was braided down the side of her head, tucked behind her ear with a hidden dagger holding it together. She wore enchanted leather armor on her body that subtly displayed her curves and emphasized the large sword on her back. On her wrist, a small crossbow was strapped that was activated by her fingers. She slapped her face and watched the blood rush in.

"I can do this," she declared to herself, "I prepared for this," and yet, her heart was still filled with fear. How could it not have been; she was returning to the place of her trauma. However, it was also the site of her greatest moment and friend.

Feeling ready, she strolled out of her room and into the camp. Unlike most of the adventurers present, Diana had stayed in the royal house in the middle of the town area. It was the place where any of the royal family stayed if they visited the dungeon area, and she had it all to herself. As she left the doorway, a shout got her attention.

"Over here your highness!"

Turning, Diana saw the small group of adventurers waiting for her. Fiora smiled at the princess as she approached.

"Nice to see that royalty wakes up at the same time as us common folk; I would have thought you'd have slept till the middle of the day."

Diana snorted and playfully punched Fiora, "I'm just glad you haven't run off into the dungeon ahead of everyone, oh fearless leader. Didn't you used to tell me how it was important to always scout ahead?"

The two fellow disciples of Mary shared a brief hug as they reunited. They shared the kind of bond one could only experience by going through a special kind of hell. Diana turned and smiled at each of the group members.

"Nic, Nat, Jonas, Gran; it is good to see you all again. I'm glad my old partner hasn't gotten any of you killed yet."

The four chuckled good-naturedly and bid their personal greetings to the princess. They had met her only a few times, but liked her and her personality.

Together, the group made their way toward the dungeon entrance, the meeting spot for Koran's group. As they approached, they saw a small number of adventurers clamoring around the rank B adventurer. Sir Koran turned and bowed to them as they approached.

"It is my great honor to welcome the princess Diana and the famous adventurer Fiora to my class for today. Welcome and I must say how pleased I am to see you alive and well princess. Why," Koran put his hand to his head and winced, "I was overcome with grief when I heard you were hurt and by my former friends no less. Rest assured princess, their families are being fully investigated at this time for their treachery."

Koran was right about the investigation, but he had failed to mention how the investigators were finding staggering amounts of suspicious material that would stall the investigations for months.

Diana smiled coolly at the bowing man, "Sir Koran, how rare it is to meet again a man of your stature and generous spirit. Why," she gestured to his class, "I can feel their strength from here. I cannot believe they are new adventurers just starting out."

Seeing his students puff out their chests in pride, Koran laughed, "These men of mine are wonderful students. I just had to show them the true fear of death and teach them how to master it. In fact, in a few weeks I will personally be seeing to their advancement to rank E. It does me proud to see how well they are doing."

The adventurers all smiled and nodded together, a slight red tingle in their eyes visible for just a moment.

Fiora eyed the men surrounding Koran, "I admit that they are indeed strong enough to advance, but isn't it much too fast? Your classes are only now approaching the end of their first week, yet you seem to think they have enough experience to advance?"

Koran coughed and smiled at her, "My dear, forgive my rudeness, but I know my students quite well. Even if they are not ready in a few weeks' time, I'll be sure they are prepared within the month."

She nodded, approving his words, "It's nice to see how well you've grown Sir Koran. It'll be an honor to serve with them once they become higher ranks."

Koran smiled, "I look forward to that day; now, enough wasting time guys; it is time to enter the dungeon." He turned dramatically, allowing the rising sun to reflect off his majestic form as he entered the dungeon with his class following eagerly.

Fiora rolled her eyes as she followed them with her group. Diana paused before she entered and turned her head to gaze up above the entrance at the rock. She stared at it, not knowing why she did so.

"Diana, hurry up now!" Fiora called out from within the cave.

Startled, Diana broke from her trance and hurried in, calling out "I'm on my way."

***

Claire watched silently as the black-haired human hurried into the dungeon. Doc hadn't picked up on her presence yet, and Claire doubted that he ever would until she neared his core. She sighed to herself.

"It was inevitable she'd return." She thought sadly, "I have mixed feelings over this, but I guess its fine for now." Musing to herself, she flew down her path as she took in the rest of the group. Both were familiar to her; the leading group had often appeared and fought for experience while the lagging group fought for rewards. So far, neither one had gone past the new first floor yet; though both were capable from her experience with them.

That wasn't what drew her attention, however. She had had her eyes on the first group ever since they entered the first time. She recognized the leader from his initial exploration of the dungeon, but something was different. Every time they entered, she picked up the barest hint of foreign magic. Normally, she wouldn't bat an eye at a mage entering the dungeon, except that whoever this one was hid their magic very well. She had yet to identify the magic user, but knew he was there.

Something about the hint of magic nagged her instincts uncomfortably, but not enough to send Doc a warning. Today, however, it seemed that the two groups had joined together to reach the depths of her partner's dungeon. It would be interesting to see them try, especially against all the new slimes that had appeared.

Thanks to the new upgrades, slimes were evolving left and right. All four elemental slime variants had appeared to an excited Doc. He had been disappointed to learn his neutral affinity prevented the evolution of light and dark variants, but had been pleased by the fire, water, wind, and earth slimes.

The elemental slimes were not very interesting in their primary form. All that occurred after evolution was a color change and an increase in resistance to a particular element. Sure the fire slimes occasionally breathed a puff of fire and the wind slimes sometimes floated a finger-length off the floor, but nothing attack related or interesting.

The big change in the slime hierarchy had come from the three special slimes. Some of the mimicry slimes had evolved into bug slimes, an offshoot that permanently held the form of a bug. While they lost their transforming abilities, they had gained some interesting aspects as a result. Their mandibles and mouth parts hardened to the point of inflicting damage and the outer slime portion had hardened to the point that it required hard blows to reach the core.

At this moment, she noted that the group had reached the third room. The aerial room, it seemed, had been cleared by one of the faster members running through and dodging all the slimes. It was a common technique and often used to bypass the dangers of the room. She watched in amusement as the leader had one of his members feel out for the hidden path. She loved seeing adventurers struggle, especially when they died. Their deaths meant a better life for her, and she rejoiced every time.

Sighing though, she watched them easily walk through the area without any problem. She left before they met the overslime, knowing full well that they would easily defeat it. Instead, she wandered down to the third floor to check on the other new slimes.

Some of the grey slimes had evolved into armor slimes after eating enough of their namesake. They were still grey, but were much larger and harder to kill with anything physical due to the hardened bits of slime and armor that floated within them and around their core.

A few grey slimes had gotten big enough to begin roaming the halls on their own. This form was a gelatinous slime, the form Doc had eagerly been awaiting for quite some time. These large blobs frequently opened what looked like a mouth as they searched for prey to envelop. They were, for all intents and purposes, immune to physical damage due to their highly viscous nature and the loss of core within their body. However, they had developed the unfortunate tendency to burn at the slightest hint of fire.

The last slime was actually an odd evolutionary form of the herb slime. Somehow, it shrunk and gained a light red complexion, gaining the name of heal slime. Heal slimes had no offensive capability and did not feed on anything alive or dead. They seemed to run on mana, and had developed the ability to heal other slimes by using the mana within them. The jungle slime boss always had two heal slimes in case of emergencies.

As Claire flew through the tunnels, a roar of pain and anger burst over her connection. Wincing, she turned quickly toward her babies.

"Momma... enemy!" The twins were trying to talk, but their emotions hindered their connection and Claire found she could not hear them.

"What's going on? What happened?" Doc spoke up now, alert and worried for their children. It was rather cute how quick he adapted.

"I don't know, but something has happened." Claire responded with a worried tone. She had only been checking on the slimes for a short time. Had the group moved so quickly in such a short time? She flew up with Doc's awareness to the twin's room.

They found the group celebrating their victory over the still bodies of the twins. Even if the girls would soon revive, Claire and Doc winced at the broken and twisted bodies as they began to fade into dungeon light.

"We should keep an eye on them," Claire muttered nervously. Her instincts once again began to knock on her heart.

***

Diana breathed out in relief as the second worg died. It had been a very intense fight for her, though not as terrifying as she thought it could have been.

In the end, their group was much too strong for the dungeon. Instead of a small group that served as the usual size in the dungeon, their large group was simply too good at overpowering obstacles in their path. During the first boss fight, they had simply surrounded the overslime and blasted it to death from afar. When it moved forward, that part of the circle had moved back while the other side moved forward. A simple, yet cunning plan she had not expected from Koran.

As she rested on the wall, one of the students walked up to her. "Are you okay princess? You didn't get hurt, did you?" The man, not much more than a boy really, asked her with a concerned tone.

"I'm fine, Simon, really I am." She said smiling, "Worry more about your friends than me; after all, they were the ones to who soaked up most of the damage."

Simon smiled at her and chuckled, "Those meat-heads didn't feel a thing, and if they did it just gives them another excuse to show off their scars."

Diana laughed with him as they observed the men clumsily bandaging their arms. Diana had been worried when the men had recklessly charged the worgs and taken their attacks, but they seemed to be fine and relatively uninjured.

"Still, I better go over there and help them with their care-taking; it's kind of painful to watch them try to wrap their..."

Simon grabbed her arm and, for a moment, Diana thought she saw anger in his eyes. She blinked, and she saw humor on his face. "Come on now princess, you know as well as I do that men don't like to be weak in front of women. Let them struggle; it's good for them."

Diana frowned and pulled her arm out of his grip, "Please remember to not touch me so casually."

Before Simon could say anything, Koran appeared between them and smiled at Diana as he pulled Simon close, "Is this one bothering you princess? I apologize for his behavior; after all, he was a sheep herder only a few days ago and doesn't know quite yet how to treat royalty. I beg your forgiveness."

Diana eyed Koran and nodded, "I understand and forgive him. Perhaps that can be something you teach him in the future?"

"Of course your highness; now if you'll excuse us." He wheeled Simon around and the two walked back to their group. Diana continued to watch them as Fiora walked up to her, "Is something wrong your highness?"

Diana whispered, "There is something strange about Simon; he's too different from the rest of the meat heads in that group. Even the meat heads are kind of strange."

"I agree," Fiora whispered back, "They hang on to Koran's every word and have a strange unity greater than any fighting force I've ever seen."

"Let's keep an eye on them for now."

***

As they cleared the second room of the third floor, Koran took Simon off to the side and wrapped a bandage around his arm. The arm was in perfect condition.

"Master, I do not think the dungeon goes deeper than this," Koran informed him, keeping his eyes down and his smile friendly, "If it did, those wolves would most likely have been deeper."

"You are correct servant; this is most likely the final floor." Simon chuckled to himself, "I quite enjoyed killing those wolfy worgs again. The fact that they recognized me made it all the sweeter when I killed them. Remember this: always keep an enemy alive so you can have fun torturing later after you ensure it won't ruin your plans."

Koran blinked in surprise, "You let them live master?"

Simon waved his hand, "Let them live, forgot about them, it's all the same in the end. Their deaths were important to arouse suspicion in the area, and becoming dungeon bosses merely served my purpose. I want to savor killing them next time...oh, right," he laughed, "There won't be a next time."

Koran smiled and patted Simon on the back as they got back up. "When will it be time Master?"

"After we kill the dungeon."

***

Doc and Claire watched the approaching group with increasing concern. Somehow, they were unable to listen in on any conversation the group made, and it was quite obvious they were moving toward a goal.

"They are after me, aren't they?" Doc asked seriously.

Claire grimaced, "I think half of them are; the other half are merely along for the ride as they say. It may have been only two words, but I picked up that the girls really hated someone from this first half."

"Perhaps one of them was involved in the death of their pack?" Doc pointed out insightfully.

Claire grumbled as she considered, "Perhaps, but they said they smelled brimstone. We would know if a demon entered our dungeon; it would send off alarms of danger in both our heads."

"Well..." Doc paused, "Something is happening in me and has been ever since they entered."

Claire looked over in surprise, "Oh? What is it?"

Doc hummed and thought for a moment, "There were originally two feelings, but one is being drowned out by the other. I feel... hungry."

Claire nodded, "I'm surprised you haven't felt this sooner. All dungeons feel hunger."

"No, I'm really... hungry." Doc seemed to be slowing down as the group moved closer to his room.

"Doc, are you okay?" Claire asked worryingly.

In response, a tentacle shot up and tried to wrap itself around her. She shrieked and flew into the house, slamming the door behind her. Naturally, the tentacle had not been able to touch her due to their pack, but it meant Doc had really tried to eat her.

"Doc, please tell me what's wrong." Claire begged, frightened by his sudden actions. He did not respond, and Claire was left stranded inside her home as the adventurers reached the boss room. She couldn't help him anymore now.

Chapter 24

The group moved cautiously now as they neared the last room. The torch lights had gradually become dimmer the closer they got to it, casting the tunnels in strange shadows. The only noise came from the soft echo of their footsteps.

Nic gulped and poked his sister, "Sis, you've read all the reports, right? What is the identity of the new boss?"

Nat shook her head wearily, "No one has made it this far down yet because of the two worgs. Those that did defeat them were too injured to continue and retreated with the recall spell. This will be the first encounter."

Koran turned his head and nodded, "Indeed, this will be the hardest part for us. When I first entered the dungeon, the overslime actually was quite difficult until we figured out how to attack it. Since then, however, the dungeon has had plenty of time to create a more dangerous monster."

Fiora strolled up to the front of the group, "I'll inspect the room." Of course, no one denied her.

Fiora slowly poked her head into the room and looked around. The room was lit by a single torch on the back wall, and the light illuminated the plant covered walls and ceiling. She narrowed her eyes as she gazed over every surface, but could not find a hint of the boss.

"It's the plant room," she announced, "And I don't see any indication of the boss. The plants are a lot bigger though, so prepare any fire magic you may have."

The group slowly entered the room, spreading around the room to inspect the area. Still, no boss appeared to fight them.

"Maybe the boss was already defeated?" Simon asked curiously.

Jonas shook his head, "The boss rooms may not be separated into the other dimensions, but the presence of the worgs proved that we are the first to get to this level. More likely the boss has to be activated somehow."

As they mused, Simon casually leaned back into a wall. The hand holding the torch accidentally brushed the wall, burning a few leaves.

SSSSSSSKKKKKKrrrrrrreeeeeeee!

A horrible shriek filled the room, enough to force everyone to cover their ears in pain. As they flinched, something fell onto two of Koran's class. As the two inspected the goop that had fallen on them, a shadow covered them.

A huge green slime fell from the ceiling and quickly crushed the two members. They screamed for just a moment before they were enveloped by the slime. The group watched in horror as the two men quickly dissolved into bones within the slime.

The slime shook violently and coughed out the bones with a thick slime covering.

"That is a jungle slime!" Jonas cried out in amazement, "They are poisonous and have some control over plants. Make sure to avoid the spikes; they can be launched from its body."

As they formed up lines, Diana's eyes were drawn to the slime-covered bones. They seemed to be twitching in the dim light.

"Jonas, the bones are moving!" She cried out in fear.

Jonas cursed, "The slime was filled with plant matter. It can use the bones to form minions!"

As he announced this, the bone slimes rose up and began to sluggishly move forward toward their shield wall. Koran cursed as he watched his former students rise against him, "Mage, what kind of attacks do they have?"

"They can spread their condition through skin to skin contact, but since they are essentially plants fire will work well." Jonas fired a fireball at the closer goo zombie. It lit up and fell back under the force of the slime, and tried to get back up.

"Lookout!" Gran warned, "The boss is moving!"

The boss turned and fired three spikes at the group. Koran braced his shield and blocked one of them while Fiora deflected the second. Another student tried to block the third spike, but his lowly wooden shield blew apart as his body was launched backwards into the wall. The man turned green and died from the poison before even landing on the ground. Nat threw an oil canister on him and lit it as he slid down.

"Burn anyone who dies to the poison!" she yelled as the body lit up, "We don't want any of them to come back as enemies while we're fighting!"

Fiora split her group from Koran's, taking them to the far side of the boss. Nic and Nat joined her in slashing at the boss with their swords while Gran and Jonas fired from the back. Koran attacked the slime from the other side, using his long sword to cut the spikes he could reach off as they began to regrow. Simon called out orders to the remaining students, who used scrolls to temporarily enchant their blades with fire. They sliced at the two goo zombies and tried to cut off their slime.

Diana joined Fiora's group in the background, firing her little crossbow at the slime. "This is wrong," She muttered to herself as she fired again and again, "Something is wrong with the dungeon."

The boss roared out and began to spin rapidly. Koran cursed and cried out, "Look out! It's using its special skill!" He threw himself to the ground with his shield covering him as the slime launched all of its spikes in every direction.

Fiora and Nic managed to dodge the spikes, but Nat was knocked back by a glancing blow. She let out a "oomph" as she spun to the floor and gasped in pain.

"Sister, are you all right?" Nic asked fearfully.

Nat cursed as she inspected herself, "Bloody thing nicked me with its damn spike. I think a little poison got in me."

Jonas, hearing this, immediately cast a lesser heal on her. He didn't specialize in healing, but he did know a little. Nat cursed as she got back up, "That helped, but I still feel it moving inside me. Let's hurry and kill it so I can get a real damn healer to help me."

"You're welcome, you arrogant bitch!" Jonas retorted as he shot another fireball at the slime. A cry of fear alerted them to the other side of the room.

Two students were killed by the spikes and had promptly melted in goo on the ground. Thankfully, the goo was inert and not attacking them; but the shield line was distracted and broken. One of the goo zombies managed to sink a hand onto one of the members, who moaned in pain as the slime quickly covered his body and dissolved him into bones. The new goo zombie turned and dissolved its former fellow.

"Get back you guys!" Simon cried out, "Reform the lines and don't let them touch you!" The four remaining students lined up and resumed slashing at the three goo zombies, but displayed less success than before.

Cursing, Koran turned from the boss and charged the zombies. "Take this Flaming Slash!" His sword burst into flame as Koran sliced through all 3 zombies and destroyed them. Before anyone could congratulate him, he slumped to the floor and panted in exhaustion.

"Huh, huh, I need a few minutes to recover," he panted out, "That skill uses a lot of my mana and stamina. You lot, attack the boss and assist Fiora!"

His students nodded and threw themselves at the dungeon slime boss now.

As if sensing the demise of its minions, the jungle slime roared again and slapped the ceiling with a tentacle. To everyone's surprise, two little light red slimes landed on the boss's body.

"Jonas, I need an identity on those slimes!" Fiora shouted as she sliced a re-growing spike away.

"I don't know." Jonas replied, "I've never seen that type of slime in my books."

"Fricking useless mage," Nat muttered, "Can't you do anything right?"

Jonas gave her a stink eye as he shot another fireball at the boss. "The poison is messing with your mind, but I'll be sure to pay you back for this later."

As the jungle slime reeled back from their attacks, the two little slimes began glowing. As they glowed, the adventurers watched as the jungle slime began to regrow parts of itself.

"Those are fricking healing slimes!" Nat cursed loudly, "Someone shoot them off the boss!"

Gran, pulled is bow back and launched two arrows at each little slime, but they missed when the boss began to rotate again.

"Not again," Simon groaned, "It's firing once more!"

One of the lower spikes managed to tear through another classmate, leaving a gaping hole in his abdomen. With a groan, the man fell backwards and stopped moving.

"Get the healers while it's recovering!" Fiora commanded as she dashed back into the fight.

Gran killed one using his triple arrow skill while Jonas managed to freeze the other off into a chunk that shattered on impact with the floor. Between the two groups, the boss slowly began to shrink from their combined attacks on its body.

Diana eyed the slime as it withered down, "I think it's almost gone guys, keep it up!"

As she said that, a glint of metal distracted her eyes for a moment, but she couldn't follow it. However, a stalagmite from the ceiling fell and landed on Nic's head as he swung his sword. With a groan, he pitched forward into the slime.

"NICK!" Nat cried out in horror, but it was too late as they were forced to watch him dissolve into bones within the boss.

With cries of rage, Nat abandoned her shield and began hacking her sword into the slime like a mad woman. The boss was so distracted it couldn't spit out the bones and they also dissolved within it.

"DIE, YOU BASTARD, DIE!" Nat cried out, tears pouring down her face.

Fiora joined her, grief stricken as well at the death of one of her oldest friends. Jonas, in his fury at the death of his best friend, began channeling his mana into a larger spell that he flung forward in agony.

"Flame Lance!"

A pole comprised of flame flew forward and tore through the boss down the center. With a groan, the slime fell backwards and shuddered in apparent death throbs.

"We did it!" Diana cried out happily. Jonas, panting in exhaustion, smiled happily as the slime wiggled in front of him. He was so engrossed that he failed to dodge the dagger than pierced his side. He yelped in pain as he fell to the ground.

Fiora's group turned wildly to find Koran, Simon, and the two remaining students approaching them with their swords pointed at them. Koran grinned, "I must say what an honor it was serving with you Fiora and that I look forward to our future business together."

Nat ran over to Jonas and pulled the dagger out, quickly wrapping his injury as Gran joined her. She glared at Koran and snarled, "I should have known you would do something like this; how dare you hurt Jonas!"

Koran scoffed, "I thought you'd be angrier with how I killed Nick than your friend there."

The room froze as his words entered the ears of the adventurer group. They processed his words and slowly understood what he meant.

"You killed... him. YOU KILLED HIM!" Nat screamed in fury as she charged Koran. She ran at him with her sword swinging wildly in her hands.

However, as she approached him, Simon stood in her way. "MOVE, YOU PIECE OF SHIT BASTARD!" Nat demanded as she ran forward.

Simon smiled evilly, "I think not my dear. I have need of you." As she neared him, Simon gracefully dodged her sword and grabbed Nat's head in both hands. Her momentum stalled, she glared into the eyes of the one who stopped her. As she did so, her eyes lost their focus as she slumped forward to the ground.

"What did you do to her?" Fiora demanded, taking a stance between them and the three other members of her group.

Simon chuckled, "Why, I merely helped her through her anger. Isn't that right Natalie?"

Nat slowly got up off the ground, but turned toward her friends rather than Koran. Her eyes glowed red as she pointed her sword in their direction.

"Nat, snap out of it! What did you do?" Jonas managed from the floor.

Simon grinned, "As I said, I helped her through her anger. See, those who possess hearts in pain desire to rid themselves of the pain. I remove that pain and control it, leaving me with perfect vessels for my biding."

Gran, his normally handsome features hardening, growled out, "You are no human. What are you?"

Simon grinned as his form blurred and changed. Instead of a young man standing before them, a red skinned monster with large teeth and four arms loomed in front of them.

Jonas gasped out, "That is a demon of wrath, known for their destructive powers and ability to control anger and fury."

The demon bowed to Jonas, "I am pleased to see that word of my noble kind is still passed down in your society. Sadly, Jonas, I have no need for a magic user in my plans. There is also the fact that I hate your kind."

Jonas chuckled, wincing at the pain it caused, "Afraid that I may bind you and return you to your home dimension, creature? Just give me a moment and I will do so."

The demon let out a wicked laugh as it pointed ahead. The two students and Nat started moving forward toward them. "I know you are not well-versed in summoning foolish mage. Neither was the foolish summoner who called me in the first place, and I made sure to completely devour his essence."

The demon turned to Diana, "Why, he was so full of anger and hate I just had to oblige him. Wouldn't you agree, sister?"

And the demon changed forms again, this time revealing a form that filled Diana with horror.

Marcus Duran smiled at his sister with a sinister grin. "Have you no desire to hug your brother?" He taunted, opening his arms out in a friendly manner.

"You are the one who tried to kill me." Diana said in shock, almost falling to the ground.

Marcus shrugged, "I just needed you in pain, not dead. It was too bad those bubbling idiots almost ruined everything with their mistake. Still, everything else has gone according to plan so far."

"The worg massacre and murders in the camp; those have been your doing." Fiora realized in horror.

Gran nodded, "The more pain he causes the more control this kind of demon can exert. From his power, I guess this is one of the strongest in the demon hierarchy." Gran frowned at Marcus, "Your goal is the royal family."

"Of course it is," the demon declared as his servants closed the distance, "Once I stop the rampage of the mad sister who killed all her family, I'll take the throne in grief. The kingdom will be filled with sorrow and anger as I summon my brethren and we will have a foothold in this world."

Something clicked in Diana, "You want the power of the dungeon; you want to eat the heart crystal."

Marcus frowned, "Enough of this, I just need you to wait patiently as I gain the power I need. Then, none of you will be able to resist me."

Diana drew her sword and stood next to Fiora, "Over my dead body."

Marcus growled, "You may be a part of my plan, but I don't strictly need you alive after this. Surrender or perish like your former brother."

"I refuse," she retorted, "I won't help you with you plan dead or alive."

"It's amazing how intact you are," he mused to himself, "At any other time I would flay you to learn your secret, but I've wasted enough of that already."

Marcus grinned and gestured, "Koran, go help subdue our guests."

Koran, grinning madly, walked up to join the servants.

"You traitor; how could you join that thing?" Fiora spit.

"Power and money my fair lady," he chuckled, "Also the promise of you and your mentor in my bed once this is all over. I'll be sure to cherish each moment till I tire and get rid of you to the whorehouses."

Fiora and Diana braced themselves as Gran drew his bow from behind them.

***

...

...

...

... Hungry.

...

...

... Dangerous.

...

... Kill.

...

... Mmmmiiinnneeee.

***

As the servants closed in on the adventurers, a shudder shook the dungeon. Marcus frowned, "What is that racket?"

Before anyone could react, two spikes shot out and obliterated the remaining former students. Everyone whirled around to find the jungle slime wiggling up and moving quickly toward them.

Marcus frowned in annoyance, "Stay dead you stupid blob." He raised his hand and launched multiple fireballs at the slime. The slime shuddered under every blow, but continued regardless. Marcus's face drew back into a feral snarl.

"KNOW YOUR PLACE AND PERISH! OBEY ME!" His fury peaked as he created lances of flame and shot them through the boss. The boss finally stopped moving and began dissolving rapidly. Marcus huffed in annoyance.

"Really, now? A mere slime made me that angry? I must be getting soft in this realm." He turned back, "Now that that's finally finished…"

He paused as he tried to move his foot and failed. He looked down to find thick vines wrapping his legs to the ground. He rolled his eyes, "A last attempt to devour me I suppose. I only need a little flame to…"

"Thunk"

Everyone stared at the crossbow bolt embedded in Marcus. Jonas smiled as Diana's abandoned crossbow slipped from his fingers. "I got you, you arrogant son of a bitch."

Marcus froze as he stared at his chest. As a trickle of blood began coming out of the wound, his face morphed into a fusion of Marcus and the demon's.

"Die." It was one word said at room volume, but it held the repressed fury of a thousand acts of denial. A white fireball flew forward toward Jonas with a speed that left no one able to react.

Everyone except the princess.

Diana took the full force of the blast for Jonas and slammed into the wall in the far back. She gave a little gasp as her life left her body.

***

.... MINE! MINE! MINE! MINE!

MINE MINE MINE MINE MINE MINE!

HANNAH!!!!!!!!!!!!!!!!!!!!!!

The dungeon began vibrating wildly as everyone struggled to gain their footing.

Marcus cursed loudly, "How?! This violates the agreement, the dungeon cannot directly interfere!"

As if in answer, everyone heard a small twinkling voice in their heads.

"Foolish demon, the accord was broken when you killed the dungeon's possession. By slaying his chosen avatar, you have brought ruin on to your very being."

Marcus paled as he slowly backed away, "No, no, no! I won't let this be the end of my plans!" With a cry, he fled down the tunnel away from the room.

"Master! Wait for me!" Koran dashed after his master as the dungeon shook.

Without his presence, Nat collapsed like a puppet without a master. Fiora ran and caught her before she fell.

"Brave adventurers, you are permitted to leave this place." The voice said in their ears, "Take your earned rewards and leave this matter while the dungeon is distracted by his prey. If you do not leave quickly, it will devour you where you stand as well."

Fiora turned to stare sadly at Diana's still body, "We need to take her with us."

"That is not permitted. All who die within the dungeon belong to my lord. Know that the demon will not bother you again; you may inform your guild of that."

"Who are you?" Gran asked as he lifted Jonas over his shoulder.

The voice seemed to twinkle in amusement, "I am a mere servant, the same as any who belong to the dungeon. Know that the next time you enter, your lives will once again be forfeit."

With that, Fiora nodded and activated the recall spell. The four remaining adventurers disappeared in a flash of light from the boss room.

Claire flew out and inspected Diana's body. "Child, he may never know why but you are now connected with him." She smiled and kissed her body, "I look forward to seeing you again noble princess." She stayed and watched as the body of Diana shimmered and disappeared into a thousand little lights.

***

The demon ran as fast as he could through the dungeon tunnels, cursing with every step. "I almost had it in my grasp. This will set me back for years, but I will take my place as prince of the wrath demons." He came across a divide and ran down the right path.

As he ran, a thought occurred to him.

There were no dividing paths from the direction of the boss's room.

His foot fell through a pitfall and he slammed his chin into the other side as he fell down the hole. Dazed, he shook his head as he picked himself up. A slurping sound emanated around him as he realized the size of the hole he had fallen into.

"Bastards, I will not die from petty slimes!" He cried out, his form covered in a layer of fire.

The slimes around him backed off and fled from the flames. Marcus laughed, "Ha, ha, ha! I have nothing to fear from you, inferior creatures!"

A red slime slowly made its way behind him and leaped onto his back. Marcus stumbled forward and landed on the ground.

"Little annoyance, why... you... my fire!"

The fire around the demon disappeared into the slime as it devoured it. Marcus paled completely.

"An infernal slime." he whispered. The bane of his race, long extinct after it was hunted by his tribe. It devoured flame as food and was immune to it as well.

Without the fire, Marcus was only a stronger being than a human. Strength, however, did not matter in this dungeon.

As the other slimes closed in on him, he let out a final scream of rage and hate.

... And the slimes fell upon him in droves.

Koran heard his master's dying screams as he ran away. He knew the dungeon was focused on him now, making his own escape a certainty.

"I'll have to leave the country after this mess." He muttered angrily, "Thankfully I have friends in other cities." He was already thinking about his future crimes when a tentacle tripped him to the floor.

He jumped up and took his sword out, looking for his assailant. "Show yourself!" He demanded.

A girlish giggle echoed around him, sending a shiver down his spine.

Koran swung his body around as he searched for the voice, his sword cutting through the air as his fear grew.

"SHOW YOURSELF!" He demanded again.

A form jiggled into his view from the darkness. It moved slowly across the ground and forced Koran back against the wall. When he couldn't move anymore, the slime grew up and adopted a familiar form.

Koran paled at the figure in front of him, "It can't be; you're dead! YOU ARE DEAD!"

The voice giggled again; it was the figure of Diana smiling at him. She cocked her head at him, and then slowly began to move forward with purpose.

Koran began to swing his sword wildly at the approaching slime, slicing small pieces of her off. The slime Diana frowned and backed up as she retracted her body protectively, eyeing the sword in front of her. As Koran began to calm down, tentacles wrapped around his body and squeezed, forcing him to drop his blade in pain.

He paled as the tentacles began to drag him back toward the terrifying slime. He screamed and struggled with all his might, begging and screaming apologies and threats. The slime paid him no mind as she slowly absorbed him in a large hug.

She smiled sweetly at Koran, before her mouth opened impossibly wide and devoured his entire body. She giggled as he felt him screaming inside her. Her blue form slithered back into the darkness, taking her victim with her out of the light.

Epilogue

Mary sighed as she reread the report in front of her. She tilted her head up to gaze into the former pupil's eyes. "So, is this everything that happened?"

Fiora nodded, stiff faced and sad, "Yes, it is as I have told it. At some point, Prince Marcus attempted a demon summoning for unknown reasons. As he was not a practiced summoner of any level, the demon devoured him, body and soul. It used his intellect and cunning to come up with a plan to turn the city into a demon controlled land and masqueraded as the prince."

"It enlisted the help of the former sir Koran to drag people into emotional compromise and took control of them. It also shape-shifted into various monsters to cast suspicion on the dungeon and other local monsters in order to send more people into despair and fury. The two, however, failed to break the noble princess and convert her into a demonic disciple. The princess sacrificed her life in the dungeon to make sure we escaped them so we could not recover the body."

Mary nodded, "What of the voice you heard in the dungeon? Do you have any inkling toward its identity?"

Fiora shook her head, "I do not."

Mary nodded as she tapped on an orb sitting on her desk. A picture of a forest pixie appeared on it. "What you heard was a dungeon pixie; a rare variant of pixie that lives within the dungeon. They somehow bond with the crystal and live their lives in willing servitude to the dungeon. Very little is known about them because they cannot survive without their partner. The few that were captured expired after a few days and never said a word. They only talk to adventurers in extreme situations within the dungeon."

Mary leaned forward, "She called Diana the avatar, is that correct?"

"Yes, but what does that mean?" Fiora asked curiously, "It frightened the demon into fleeing and the dungeon rumbled like an earthquake."

Mary sighed and leaned back, tears gathering over her eyes. "It means the dungeon chose her, and she chose it. Before she left, she confided in me that she had stabilized as a disciple, but did not know who she had bonded with. Obviously, she had paired with the dungeon and became its avatar. Avatars are legendary figures in our history; they bridge the gap between dungeon and the other races. The greatest dungeon cities of our time only came about due to the dungeons' avatars making the dungeons cooperate with the inhabitants. In theory, dungeons are the deities of their dungeon and can bond with humans and others if they so choose; but almost all prefer to eat all who enter. It is quite a shame Diana perished so soon before she could accomplish her duties. "

"Still," Mary clenched her fists as a sadistic smile came over her, "Slaying an avatar is forbidden, especially within the dungeon itself. When one slays an avatar, it invites the pure rage of the dungeon, which will not stop until the perpetrators are dead. That was learned long ago, after enough deaths occurred from such mistakes. The demon may have escaped back to its home plane, but it will be severely weakened for many centuries. We will never see it or Sir Koran again."

Fiora smiled wryly, "I guess that's a good thing then. What do you think the responses of the nobles will be?"

Mary groaned and dumped her head on the table, "When this gets out, the church will lead an inquisition as you have never seen. With one of the two princes dead, the succession has been decided, but Father Tobias will have the authority to investigate every level of government and guild for demon corruption. At least he is a reasonable man, but there will still be many changes before he is satisfied the area is cleansed. You and your group will most likely be promoted a rank, a small comfort to your loss."

"Nic is sorely missed." Fiora admitted, "Natalie is stricken with grief and poison while Jonas watches over her. I only hope the flame he carries for her will save her from her pain. Gran has left to report to his elders, and I'm here with you."

Mary sighed and picked herself back up, "Indeed, this is a disaster for everyone. Go home and rest Fiora, you deserve that much before the questioning begins." As Fiora closed the door behind her, Mary let the tears she had been holding back fall down her face. Her blood connection to Diana had long since vanished, and she had lost another friend.

***

Michelle sighed as she packed her bags. "Such a disappointment, I really thought he could do it."

"I'm really surprised too big sis." Shelly piped up from her side of the tent, "We gave that silly prince a duke level demon summoning book and it still failed in the end."

Michelle turned and tussled her little sister's hair, "It goes to show that our summoned relatives are less than us little one. Then again, summoning from the fury circle is always a risk; we should have asked one of our relatives from the lust circle."

Shelly giggled, "If that happened, then we couldn't have used our powers to control it, silly big sis."

"Right you are, munchkin. Now, hurry and pack; we don't want to be here when those church dogs begin sniffing around."

Shelly sniffed sadly, "Are we leaving for good big sis? I really liked exploring the dungeon, and letting the men take the fall for us. If we go home, I'll be so bored again." She pouted, her crooked tooth morphing into a perfect smile.

"Patience my little sister," Michelle knelt down and hugged her, her hair changing into a blonde wave down her back, "We can't go home remember? They banished us for embracing our heritage."

Shelly giggled, "I thought it was because we tried to take over the kingdom and bring back the demon lords? The disciples really didn't like us trying to corrupt them, right?"

"There was that as well," Michelle admitted, "In any case, the dungeon has proved itself to be a formidable force, one that we can use at a later date. That fool duke did teach us that our glamour won't work the deeper we go into the dungeon; it senses us and hungers for our power."

"Is that why they say dungeons are related to demons?" Shelly asked curiously.

"Only to those of the gluttony circle little sister, and no one has been able to prove that. We leave for now, but we'll not go too far and we'll come back after the church is gone. Let's think of a new plan while we wait."

"Can we use men still?"

"Of course, sweetie; I'd never deny your instincts. Let's go find us some bag carriers and someone to lend a wagon. In fact, let's invite all of them to come with us. Traveling always makes me hungry."

For just a moment, red wings and a black tail appeared on the sisters, but perhaps it was just a trick of the light in the tent.

Made in the USA
Middletown, DE
31 July 2017